It won't hurt a bit.

Sharon studied Jackie with a critical frown. "You know what's wrong? Your face is too small for all this hair. You need your eyebrows plucked. That'll open up your eyes, make them look bigger." She began rooting in her tote bag for tweezers.

"No wait — "

"Close your eyes," Sharon ordered. "Don't flinch. I'll pull each hair in the direction it's growing. It won't hurt a bit."

Either Sharon's sense of direction was off or the tweezers were dull because Jackie couldn't remember when she'd been in such agony. As Sharon wrenched each hair, tears of pain streamed from Jackie's eyes, and she sneezed violently after each extraction.

Sharon mumbled something about having to remove a couple more to "even them up." At last she put the tweezers down. "Don't look yet. I have to get my eyebrow pencil."

Jackie's eyes flew open. The image that stared back at her in the mirror looked surprised. No wonder. She had no eyebrows left. *None.* "Sharon!" she screamed. "I don't have any eyebrows!" She burst into tears.

"It's not as bad as it looks," Sharon said hastily. "Don't get upset. I'll lend you my eyebrow pencil until your eyebrows grow back in. I'm really sorry, Jackie. I kept trying to even them up and — well . . . I'm still new at this."

"You ruined me!" Jackie cried.

Other Apple Paperbacks
by CANDICE F. RANSOM
you will enjoy:

My Sister, the Meanie
My Sister, the Traitor
Millicent, the Magnificent

MY SISTER THE CREEP

Candice F. Ransom

AN
APPLE
PAPERBACK

SCHOLASTIC INC.
New York Toronto London Auckland Sydney

No part of this publication may be reproduced in whole or in part, or stored in a retrieval system, or transmitted in any form or by any means, electronic, mechanical, photocopying, recording, or otherwise, without written permission of the publisher. For information regarding permission, write to Scholastic Inc., 730 Broadway, New York, NY 10003.

ISBN 0-590-41529-8

Copyright © 1989 by Candice F. Ransom. All rights reserved. Published by Scholastic Inc. APPLE PAPERBACKS is a registered trademark of Scholastic Inc.

12 11 10 9 8 7 6 5 4   1 2 3 4 5/9

Printed in the U.S.A.   40

First Scholastic printing, May 1990

To Frank, my forever-friend

Chapter 1

The day her sister was scheduled to leave for college, Jackie Howard was eagerly helping Sharon with last-minute clean up. Jackie really didn't like housekeeping that much; she had an ulterior motive. The instant her sister left, she planned to transfer her belongings from her room to Sharon's.

Boxes and suitcases stood outside in the hall, making it difficult for anyone to walk through the house. After lunch, Mr. Howard would load everything into their car, and the whole family would drive Sharon to Harrisonburg, a hundred miles west of their Fairfax, Virginia, home.

Sharon was anxious to go. On her hands and knees, she tossed papers and old shoes from the bottom of her closet with gleeful abandon. "I can't believe it, Jackie. In a few more hours I'll be free! My own person!"

"Can I have this?" Jackie asked. In her task of cleaning out Sharon's bottom dresser drawer, she had turned up some interesting items. She held a rhinestone hair clip in two fingers. "You probably won't have room for it."

Sharon withdrew from the closet to see what Jackie had found. "I might still use it."

"You can't take everything." Jackie fastened the clip in her ponytail. Now that her hair was growing, she could wear bows and barrettes. Sharon's cast-offs would be ideal, though her sister seemed reluctant to part with so much as a bent bobbypin.

Jackie had been counting heavily on Sharon's leaving behind a few choice items, like her stereo and portable TV. No such luck. Even when Mrs. Howard argued that Sharon's roommate would also bring a record player and TV and that dorm rooms were *tiny*, Sharon refused to give up a single possession. The stereo and TV, along with a crate of record albums, enough clothes to stock a department store, and a ton of makeup, costume jewelry, and shoes were going with Sharon, even if it meant she had to sleep curled up in a bathtub.

"Put the hair clip in the Maybe pile," Sharon said to Jackie.

Frowning, Jackie unclipped the barrette and tossed it into the middle pile on Sharon's bed. The Maybe pile was almost as big as the Definitely pile. Both contained by far the best stuff.

2

The Forget It pile, at the end of the bed, was slated for the trash or Jackie, depending on her sister's generosity. The selection in this pile was the dregs — an old algebra book, a compact with a cracked mirror, holey tennis shoes, and a bold-faced carnival doll dressed entirely in plumes, a prize won by Sharon's senior year boyfriend. Sharon's cat, one possession that was staying behind, chewed a tuft of pink feathers, his paw across the doll's neck as if to keep it from running away.

"You're not leaving me *any*thing," Jackie protested, glancing around at the stripped room. "I'm surprised you're not taking the light bulbs and the nails from the floor."

"Jackie, I'm going away forever." Sharon pitched a bunch of school papers at the trash can and missed. "I need all these things."

"You'll be back at Thanksgiving. And Christmas. And probably next summer."

"But only to visit." Sharon pointed to a felt banner tucked behind the vanity mirror. "You can have my Fairfax High pennant. And my drill team rifle. I won't need that juvvie stuff any more."

"Really? Thanks!" The pennant was nice, since Jackie would start her freshman year at Fairfax High the next week, but the fake wooden rifle was a real bonus. She had already decided to try out for the drill team. Sharon had been on the team, attaining the rank of captain in her final year. After watching her sister practice semester after semester, Jackie knew all the rou-

3

tines by heart and figured the tryouts would be a breeze.

Mrs. Howard came in to empty the overflowing trash can. "Aren't you girls finished yet? Sharon, your father wants to be on the road by three. Any later and we'll catch all that weekend traffic."

"We're almost done," Sharon said.

"I don't know why you have to go clear to Harrisonburg to school," Mrs. Howard said for the five millionth time since Sharon announced her decision.

"Mom, Madison's not that far. You act like I'm going to Alaska or something."

"You can attend beauty school right here in Fairfax." Mrs. Howard continued the discussion that had been running all summer between her and Sharon. "It would be a lot cheaper."

Money wasn't really the issue. Jackie was aware that her mother would try anything short of lying down in front of the car to keep Sharon from leaving home. Jackie couldn't wait for her sister to go, and not just so she could move into Sharon's room.

"Mom, I'm taking cosmetology courses at the beauty academy *and* courses at the university. In business," Sharon clarified. "I want to have my own salon someday, not just be a beauty operator in somebody else's shop."

"She's going to be Sharon of Hollywood," Jackie said.

Mrs. Howard made an eleventh-hour attempt

to dissuade Sharon. "Well, then, you can go to beauty school in Fairfax and take business courses at Strayer College in Washington. The bus goes right downtown."

"Like Sonny Perkins." Jackie referred to the grown son of their neighbor who lived across Lee Highway, right beside the garage the Perkinses owned. "I saw him every morning when I was in fourth grade. He waited for the Trailways on his side of the road, and I waited for my bus on my side. He wore a tie and carried a briefcase, just to go to school."

"And wound up driving his father's wrecker," Sharon snorted, flipping back her long brown hair. "I don't want to stay at home and commute to D.C. The whole idea is to get out of dumpy old Fairfax."

"Well, think about it," Mrs. Howard said, as if Sharon would actually change her mind. Sharon, who hated living in the rural part of the county so much, used to miss the bus on purpose so her rich ninth-grade boyfriend wouldn't find out she was a "country kid."

Jackie knew Sharon had other reasons for going to James Madison University in Harrisonburg. Most of her friends had been accepted there. It didn't matter a bit to Sharon that she wasn't aiming for a four-year degree like her friends. "While they're still sweating out those last two years, I'll be in Hollywood, hairstylist to the stars," Sharon maintained.

Jackie hadn't the slightest doubt in her sister's

future success. Sharon had always been different, never content to run with the pack. If anything, the pack ran with *her*.

Mrs. Howard twisted the garbage bag tie more turns than necessary. "You're still so young, Sharon. Just seventeen . . ."

"I'll be eighteen in January!" Sharon's voice echoed hollowly from the closet. "I can't help it if I graduated early. You should have thought of that when you enrolled me in school when I was five."

"Mama couldn't stand having you home another whole year," Jackie put in, laughing.

Mrs. Howard smiled. "And now I don't want you to go. It's funny, isn't it?" She sighed. "Well, you girls hurry. I'm going to put lunch on the table." She took the bulging garbage bag with her.

"I'm through, Sharon." After tossing papers in the trash can, Jackie wiped the inside of the drawer with a rag. She wanted the room to be spick-and-span when she moved in later that evening.

At last, she'd have Sharon's big four-drawer dresser and the deep closet to hang her clothes in. Her little room next door was okay, but it had only one window and a dinky closet.

It was killing Sharon, but she could not take her furniture, including the almost-new vanity table with matching mirror and stool. Jackie looked forward to sitting at the vanity and leisurely brushing her hair, the way she'd seen Sharon do a thousand times. Maybe, she mused,

6

if she stared in the mirror long enough, she might even start to resemble her beautiful sister.

Jackie ran over to see if she had grown any prettier since the notion popped into her head. The mirror showed she was as plain as ever. The uncluttered surface of the vanity, usually a mess, reminded Jackie of the time two years before when Sharon had declared war on her. The Great Sister War, as they now spoke of it, ended one snowy afternoon with Sharon's crazy idea of a truce. Friends once again, they threw old lipsticks and combs out the window, watching patterns form in the soft new snow.

Rubbing one finger thoughtfully around the beveled rim of the mirror, Jackie remembered the day the summer before when the Sister Rebellion had been born, in this very room. The girls banded together at that time, to fight for their independence. They didn't fare very well as rebels, especially when they fell in love with the same boy, but now Sharon was truly independent. In a matter of hours, her sister would begin a new life. And Jackie would be alone.

"Sharon!" she cried suddenly.

Sharon backed out of the closet, her eyes wide with concern. "What is it?"

"You're leaving!"

"Not until we get this room in shape. And I still have to pack the Definitely and the Maybe stuff — "

"No, I mean you're *leaving*!" Jackie wailed. "I don't want you to go!"

At the anguish in Jackie's tone, Sharon got up

and went over to the vanity. She put her arm around Jackie. "You knew I'd have to go someday. But I'll be back Thanksgiving. And Christmas."

"Just to visit, you said. It won't be the same," Jackie sniffed. She expected her sister to tell her she was too old to cry. They had celebrated Jackie's birthday the day before, even though she wouldn't be fourteen for three more days, so Sharon could be there.

"No," Sharon agreed solemnly. "It won't be the same."

Jackie let the tears flow. "We've always been together. Ever since I can remember, you've been here."

"That's because you're the youngest. I can remember when *you* weren't here. That was the darkest day of my life, when Mom brought you home from the hospital."

"Sharon, I'm serious." Jackie punched her sister. Surprisingly, Sharon let her get away with it. "I'm going to be all alone, and you're making jokes."

"I'm just trying to make you feel better." Sharon smiled. "Hey, how about we make a pact?"

"A pact?" Jackie wiped her eyes on her sleeve.

"Yeah. A pact to be friends forever, no matter what." Sharon retrieved a scrap of paper from the trash. "You can write it down if you want. You like things in writing." From her purse, Sharon produced a pen.

Jackie hesitated. "I never wrote a pact before. What'll I say?"

" 'We, the undersigned,' " Sharon dictated, " 'do hereby declare we will be friends through thick and thin, in sickness or in health, for richer or poorer — ' "

Jackie scribbled the statement, giggling. " ' — until death do us part,' " she concluded with a flourish. She signed her name and handed the pen to her sister. Sharon's signature went beneath hers. Jackie folded the document carefully. "I'll keep it in a safe place. Our friendship pact."

"The Sister Pact," Sharon corrected.

They stared at each other in the vanity mirror. They had the same brown hair and eyes, yet they looked nothing alike. At that moment, Jackie felt closer than ever to her sister. Their reflected images, mutely sealing the bond between them, seemed to be connected. When Jackie shifted a little, the Jackie-half of the image appeared incomplete without the Sharon-half.

"Well," Jackie broke the spell. "Are you ready?"

"Almost." Sharon disappeared into the closet for a final inspection. "I think I've got everything . . . what's this?" There was a curious splatting noise, as if something fell and broke on the floor. Sharon flew out of the closet, her hand clamped over her mouth, and slammed the door. She was laughing and gagging at the same time.

The unmistakable odor of rotten egg hit Jackie

immediately. She put both hands over her mouth to keep from upchucking. "Arrrrgghh!" she exclaimed from behind her hands. "What did you *do*?"

Sharon was laughing so hard she could barely answer. "I found an egg — on the top shelf — and I dropped it!"

Jackie pinched her nostrils shut. "How did an egg get in your closet?" She sounded like she had the worst cold in the world. As the smell of rotten egg penetrated her clothespin grip, she began to wish she *had* the worst cold in the world.

"It was that Easter egg we thought was too pretty to get rid of. The swirly one, remember?" Sharon grabbed her pillow and smothered her face in it.

Jackie yanked tissues from a box and stuffed them up her nose. "But that was years ago! That egg must have been seven years old! Who's going to clean this up?"

"It's your room now!"

"Sharon, you — ! How can I move in here?"

Sharon fled, screaming with laughter. "Fumigate!" she flung over her shoulder.

Jackie stumbled after her sister, furious. Now she'd have to air the room out before she could move in and that might be days! Weeks! Only her sister could foil her perfect plans with a rotten egg.

Lunch was on the table, but neither Jackie nor Sharon had much appetite.

"Sharon dropped an egg that was seven years

old!" Jackie accused. "You wouldn't believe the stink in there!"

"For heaven's sake, Sharon," Mr. Howard declared, shaking his head with mild reproach. "You're going out true to form, I'll say that."

"The room will air while we're gone," Mrs. Howard reassured Jackie.

"No, it won't. That egg is still on the closet floor!"

"You don't have time to clean it up now," Mr. Howard said.

They ate quickly, then loaded the car. Sharon's belongings took up every available inch of space. Jackie sat alone in the back seat, wedged between Sharon's record player and a suitcase with sharp corners that kept jabbing her in the ribs. Sharon sat up front between their parents.

As they cruised west toward the Blue Ridge Mountains, Jackie thought about the Sister Pact she and Sharon had signed. After what Sharon did to her room, Jackie felt like ripping the document to shreds. A true friend did not stink up another friend's room.

Soon they reached Harrisonburg, a city nestled in the Shenandoah Valley. At James Madison University, they located Sharon's dorm and helped her carry in her things. Sharon's roommate hadn't arrived yet, but the dorm rang out with the voices of other girls running up and down the halls. Jackie felt a stab of envy. Sharon's life was going to be so exciting. But then she remembered the rest of her plan. *Her* life was beginning, too.

11

When it was time to go, Sharon kissed her parents good-bye. As her sister's lips grazed Jackie's cheek, Jackie could tell Sharon had already forgotten about the rotten egg. She wondered if Sharon had forgotten the Sister Pact, as well.

When she was back home again, Jackie scrubbed the splattered egg off the closet floor, with five of her father's bandanna handkerchiefs tied around her nose for smell protection. Both windows were open wide, but the odor had barely dissipated.

"I'm moving in anyway," Jackie told her mother.

Mrs. Howard was horrified. "You can't sleep in that smelly room. You'll be sick. Wait till tomorrow, at least."

But she didn't *want* to wait. "I *have* to move in," she insisted.

"Jackie, be sensible. Another day or so won't kill you. Sharon's room isn't going anywhere."

But Jackie was. Moving into her sister's bigger, better room was part of her plan to become the important Howard sister. Now that Sharon was out of the way, Jackie was free to become her own person.

The next day Jackie transferred her clothes and books to Sharon's old room, *her* new room, with only one bandanna over her nose. The place was liveable, if she breathed shallowly and inhaled through her mouth. Her mother said she was crazy but changed the linens on Sharon's bed.

Anxious to claim her room, Jackie went to bed too early and was unable to sleep. She twisted among the sheets until she felt feverish. She probably should have taken her mother's advice and waited another day.

Pushing her damp bangs off her forehead, she swung her legs over the side of the bed. It wasn't quite dark outside. Coppery June bugs pinged against the window screens. Jackie padded over to the vanity and sat down heavily.

She gazed into the dim mirror, half-expecting to see her sister's shadowy reflection instead of her own. That was silly. Sharon was in her dorm room, a hundred miles away.

Jackie went over to the closet and opened the door, her body tense with anticipation. How many times had Sharon leaped out of the closet to scare her?

But no one sprang out. Jackie reached up and tugged the pull chain attached to the light switch. Darkness retreated to the corners. Her clothes hung neatly from the pole. Something glimmered on the floor, in the back behind her shoes. Jackie stooped to pick it up. It looked like . . . it *was* a piece of eggshell. She stared at the multicolored chip on the end of her finger a few seconds. Then she put the fragment in the secret drawer of the vanity, next to the Sister Pact.

She got back into bed. Now she knew what was wrong. The room. It was hers, but it wasn't hers. Long after the smell of rotten egg was only a memory, the ghost of her sister would linger.

13

Chapter 2

To Do Today

1. Tryout for drill team
2. Join one other club (a good one)
3. Make a whole bunch of friends
4. Fix up room really cool

Jackie taped the list to her vanity mirror. Her goals looked dumb jotted on the grocery shopping notepad she'd borrowed from her mother. But Jackie liked things in writing and the list gave her confidence. She *would* be her own person.

"Here comes Jackie Howard," she told her reflection, "the *other* Howard sister." Gathering her purse and notebook, she set off to conquer high school.

Fairfax High, Jackie discovered practically the

14

minute she entered the front door, was a lot like her bedroom. It wasn't just Sharon's *old* school; it was Sharon's *school*.

Her sister had left an impression as indelible as the "Sharon" she once painted with nail polish on the shell of a box turtle the girls caught in the garden one summer, then released. The following summer, they were amazed to see the same turtle lurching over the plowed ruts, the faint pink letters still visible on his shell.

In the entrance hall of school, Jackie spotted a photograph of Sharon in the trophy case, snapped during the previous year's big game, as Sharon led the drill team through its paces. While searching for her homeroom, Jackie passed the yearbook office with its display of framed, blown-up photographs. There was Sharon again, a junior this time, captured on the steps outside in a rare pensive pose that made her look even more beautiful.

When Jackie's teachers called the roll, she thought her biggest hurdle would be getting them to shorten her name from "Jacqueline" to the nickname she preferred. Two of her three morning-class teachers asked if she was Sharon Howard's little sister. Her math teacher made no comment when Jackie replied that she was, but her science teacher glanced at her sharply, as if thinking there was clearly some genetic imbalance between the sisters.

"I know," Jackie offered weakly. "We don't look much alike."

"It's not that," Mrs. Reed said. "I was just

15

remembering how lively your sister was."

When the bell rang for lunch, Jackie trudged down to the cafeteria. Bemoaning the fact that she'd made a pact with herself to be her own person, within minutes she'd been labeled as Sharon's little sister, the unlively one.

The cafeteria was crowded and noisy. Juggling her books and a tray of food, Jackie sat down at the first empty seat she found. Across the table, a girl about her age toyed with her food.

The girl smiled at Jackie, stirring the mess on her plate. "It's terrible, isn't it? You'd think they'd serve us decent stuff the first day at least. I wish I'd gone to McDonald's."

"I didn't think we were allowed to," Jackie said hesitantly. After her crummy morning, she wasn't in the mood to strike up a conversation.

"How do you know that?"

"When they built the McDonald's next to the school, Sharon — that's my sister — said the school decided they didn't want the students to go over there for lunch."

"That's really stupid," the girl remarked. "If the school wanted us to eat here, then they should serve Big Macs instead of this slop."

Jackie giggled, warming to the girl's friendliness. "I guess that's why they put up that fence. Sharon used to ask guys in the parking lot to get her a hamburger. They'd hand it to her through the fence."

"You have a sister here?" the girl asked.

"She graduated last year. Now she's going to Madison."

The girl nodded. "My oldest brother goes there. It's his second year. But my other brother still goes here."

"You have two older brothers?" Jackie had often wished she had a brother to protect her against Sharon.

"And one younger brother." The girl made a face. "He's a pest. Wayne is neat. He's the one at Madison. Then comes Jason; he's a senior here." She lifted her nose in the air to indicate what she thought of him. "I thought my first day here would be easy with Jason to teach me the ropes, but I haven't seen him since this morning. I guess big-shot seniors don't want to be bothered with dopey little freshmen like us."

"How did you know I was a freshman?"

The girl tapped the cover of Jackie's science book. "This." Science was a required subject for ninth-graders. "Plus that lost look you have is a dead giveaway. Don't feel bad. I'm just as lost as you are! By the way, my name is Frieda Jamison."

"I'm Jackie Howard."

"I wonder if we've got any classes together. Let me see your schedule." She pulled her own schedule from her notebook.

Jackie handed Frieda her class schedule. While Frieda compared the computer print-outs, Jackie studied her. Frieda had a square, honest face framed by thick, crinkly brown hair that reminded Jackie of Brillo. Her haircut didn't help much, chopped off just below the earlobe. She wore glasses, but her eyes behind the lenses

17

were gorgeous, a grayish hazel. A thought flitted into Jackie's head. Frieda wasn't the kind of girl Sharon would be friends with. Only the most popular kids were good enough for Sharon, but Jackie wasn't so choosy.

"I have Reed for science, too," Frieda said. "First period. Jason had her — he's says she's really tough."

"My sister had her, too." Jackie didn't add Mrs. Reed's comment about how Sharon livened up her class.

"We've got PE together!" Frieda declared. "And we're in the same English class. We can sit together. I hate not knowing anybody, don't you?"

The bell rang. Lunch was over. Scraping her chair back, Frieda said, "See you fifth period. Thank heavens we won't have to dress out in gym. The teacher will probably only ask embarrassing questions today. Then we can stumble around and find our English class together. Okay?"

"Great," Jackie replied. She had made a friend, one objective on her to-do list accomplished.

Fourth period French made her feel even better. Her teacher, Adair McConnell, was as romantic-looking as his name. Adair, Jackie thought dreamily. She would always call him Adair. Not to his face, naturally, but privately. He asked the students to introduce themselves in French.

18

"Je m'appelle Jacqueline Howard," Jackie said when it was her turn.

"Jacqueline," Adair repeated, pronouncing it "Zjock-wa-leen." "A beautiful French name. You have a nice natural accent."

Jackie sensed the envy of the other girls, who were already half in love with the teacher. Well! At last she was recognized as herself, Jacqueleen Howard, with the natural French accent.

When Adair mentioned that he was the sponsor for the French Club and that he'd like to see all of them at the first meeting later that month, Jackie copied down the date and the room number. She'd planned to join the Pep Club, but it wouldn't hurt to have more than one after-school activity.

Things went sour again in PE when Jackie learned she had Sharon's old gym teacher. Miss Huff pounced on Jackie's name right away, immediately making the family connection.

"Your sister fractured her arm in basketball trying to score an extra point," Miss Huff said, looking Jackie over as if judging whether the younger sister would be as dedicated.

"Yes, I remember," Jackie said. She also remembered that Sharon hadn't been trying to score an extra point at all, but had been pushed by a girl on the other team. Sharon fell hard, wrapping her arm around the pole like a horseshoe. Of course she was a heroine. Then came the cast plastered with signatures and the little white get-well bunny from Sharon's sophomore boyfriend. Only Sharon could turn an accident into a triumph.

"Your sister was a fine athlete, a team player," Miss Huff went on.

Jackie wondered if she should salute and hum a few bars of "The Star-Spangled Banner." Frieda rolled her eyes heavenward. At least her new friend understood what it was like to stand in the shadow of an older sibling.

"What's your phone number?" Frieda asked when PE was over and they were on their way to English. She had her pen out, prepared to write it on the back of her hand.

"Why?"

"So I can call you tonight, why else?"

Since Sharon had gone away to college, the telephone had been strangely silent. For the first time in her life, Jackie had the phone to herself. She told Frieda her phone number. Soon she would have lots of friends calling, the way Sharon did.

After that strange, mixed day, it was a relief to go home. Jackie put her books on the chair by the door. The house was cool and quiet. When Sharon was around, the stereo and TV would be blasting, and Sharon would either be yakking on the phone or ransacking the refrigerator. The place was like a mausoleum.

Jackie went into the kitchen. "Mama?"

"In here." Her mother's voice came from Jackie's old room, now the spare bedroom.

Mrs. Howard was sitting on Jackie's old bed among summer clothes that needed putting away in the cedar chest and leftover items from Sharon's Maybe and Forget It piles. The spare room, Jackie noted, was fast becoming a junk room. The pages of a letter lay in her mother's lap.

"Is that from Sharon?" Jackie recognized her sister's scrawl emphatically peppered with all-capitalized words and multiple exclamation points.

"Yes. Do you want to read it?" Mrs. Howard passed the letter to Jackie.

In typical-Sharon fashion, her sister glossed over important topics, like her classes, to dwell on her roommate's faults, which were numerous, and the unfair dorm rules.

"She doesn't say anything to me," Jackie said, miffed.

"Sure she does. At the bottom of the last page."

Jackie skimmed the last page. The reference was so slight, no wonder she had missed it the first time. " 'Tell Jackie hi,' " she quoted, annoyed at having been reduced to a mere afterthought. "I'm amazed she could spare the two whole seconds it took to write that."

"Well, you know how Sharon is." Mrs. Howard creased the letter with deliberate care, as if she intended to store it in a time capsule.

"You didn't ask me how school was," Jackie said petulantly. Usually her mother was interested in such things. "It was my first day of high school," she added, in case her mother needed reminding.

"I'm sorry. I was thinking about Sharon. She doesn't like the food there at all. I hope she's getting enough to eat."

Jackie wasn't worried. Only a worldwide famine would prevent her sister from getting her daily three-squares. "I had a terrible day," Jackie began, eager to dump her troubles on her mother.

"Really?" Distracted, Mrs. Howard fingered the edges of the letter. "You know what really worries me. She mentions something about her and a couple of other girls getting an apartment off campus. Seventeen years old and wanting an apartment. That girl will be the death of me yet."

Jackie stared at her normally understanding mother. Didn't her statement about having a terrible day register? Her mother should coddle her with tea and sympathy, offer to fix her favorite supper, maybe even take her shopping. But no, she couldn't stop thinking about Sharon, the Number One Daughter, the only one who mattered.

Number Two Daughter shuffled off to her room. Even from a distance of a hundred miles, Sharon was still dominating her life.

Sharon's cat Felix padded into her room. The cat prowled Sharon's old room three or four times a day, looking for Sharon. Felix poked his nose under the dust ruffle of Jackie's bed.

"She's not there," Jackie told the cat. "She's gone. I live here now."

Felix stared at her with half-moon yellow eyes. Then he scratched his ear with his hind foot, as if finding the new tenant deficient, and padded out again.

Jackie lay down on the bed. While she simmered with resentment, an old feeling she wished she could shrug off, she realized she missed her sister, too. Stupid stuff, like the way Sharon would pop into Jackie's room and shriek, "Somebody beat you with an ugly stick!"

Or the "trick" they used to do when Jackie was little. Sharon would stand with her arms held out to one side. Jackie would grip her sister's hands as Sharon started spinning. Sharon would swing Jackie around and around, faster and faster, until Jackie's feet actually left the ground and the world whizzed by in a blur. Jackie was never afraid — not once — that her sister would let her go.

Jackie turned over so her nose was buried in the pillow. The pillowslip was fresh, but Jackie could detect the scent that was distinctly her sister's from the depths of the pillow. If she lay there long enough, she wondered, would her scent and her sister's merge until they smelled the same? Or would her scent remain separate, her own?

Jackie lay awake, as semi-darkness slowly blanketed her room, until her mother came to the door to call her to supper.

Chapter 3

"Celeste Wellington wears a different designer scarf every day," Frieda remarked. "Her family must be rich."

"Her sister will probably be homecoming queen this year," said Paula Farquarson. "She's the one who started the fad."

Jackie took out the letter she had written Sharon in homeroom. She had brought her good stationery to school — pink with a picture of kittens in a basket — so she could copy over the letter during lunch. Even though Sharon had only scribbled a line at the bottom of the letter to their mother, Jackie had lots of things to tell her sister.

"My mom told me I could borrow her silk scarf, but it doesn't have a designer's signature on it," said Carol Lewis. A scarf without the name of a well-known designer was utterly worthless.

"I've been saving," lamented Frieda, "but by the time I have enough money, nobody will be wearing scarves anymore."

"With my allowance, the only signature I can afford will be F. W. Woolworth," Jackie said, beginning the second page of Sharon's letter. Everybody laughed and Jackie felt good.

At last she belonged to a crowd. Not a very big crowd and certainly not a group other kids were clamoring to get into, but a crowd just the same. Both Carol Lewis and Paula Farquarson were in Jackie's and Frieda's gym class. They were all leftovers or, as Miss Huff called them, substitutes — a polite term that didn't disguise the fact that no one wanted them when the hockey teams were formed.

Carol Lewis was on the yearbook staff. She had long, no-color hair she wore parted in the middle, which only drew attention to her potato-like nose. Paula was blonde and cute, but she always reminded Jackie of the nursery song, "I'm a little teapot, short and stout."

The girls were nice, but it bothered Jackie that they seemed content to languish in the gray area of semi-losers. None of them could be classified as out-and-out losers, like the tough girls who hung around the greasers and laughed like seagulls. They didn't scuttle around the halls like the mousy girls who were obsessed with the Computer Club. And they definitely weren't popular like the cheerleaders and other movers and shakers who controlled the freshman class.

They weren't anything, just struggling ninth-grade girls, we'll-stick-together-and-get-through-this-somehow friends. Jackie didn't want to barrel through her freshman year as if it were an obstacle course. Or medicine to be swallowed without tasting. She wanted to hurl herself into high school life the way Sharon did, join the Pep Club, try out for the drill team, have *fun*.

"Even if a fad got started and we already had whatever it was, nobody would notice," Frieda grumbled. She did this a lot, about everything, the food, the classes, her teachers.

Frieda Jamison directed their little group as an unofficial leader. Jackie realized that Frieda collected strays, people who didn't fit in anywhere. She didn't want to be one of Frieda's strays.

"Have you thought about joining one of the clubs?" Jackie suggested, attempting to divert her onto a more pleasant subject.

Frieda readily switched to a new set of complaints. "I was in French Club last year. It was so dumb. All we did was learn to read a menu in French, and at the end of the year we went downtown to Le Canard restaurant — that's "the duck" in French. They had nine kinds of duck. I ordered duck with turnips, only I didn't know that's what I was getting because I translated wrong. Before that we ate escargots. Snails! Talk about gross!"

"What about trying out for cheerleading? Or the drill team?" Jackie suggested.

26

"Only the cool kids are picked for those," Frieda said with the sour-grapes authority of someone who had no chance on either team. "Anyway, the cheerleaders are all snobs. And I wouldn't be caught dead on the drill team. That's just for the rejects who can't make cheerleaders."

Jackie's tone was chilly. "My sister was captain of the drill team last year."

"I didn't mean your *sister*," Frieda amended hastily. "I heard that *some* of the girls who tried out for cheerleaders got on the drill team."

"Well, I'm going to try out," Jackie said.

"You are?" Carol asked, impressed that one of them was going to brave something as risky as drill team tryouts.

"I know the routines by heart. Sharon was on the team for three years. I can twirl the rifle pretty good." Actually, she hadn't put her name on the sign-up sheet yet. She wanted to, but she was afraid. Maybe she was more of a stray, content to be restricted to the Gray Area, than she wanted to admit.

"We'll come down and watch you try out," Paula said.

"And cheer really loud when it's your turn," Carol added staunchly.

"You, too?" Jackie asked Frieda.

"Hey, would I let a friend down?" In a pinch, Frieda could always be counted on.

Jackie was glad. Maybe her friends weren't the kind of girls Sharon would associate with, but she was grateful for them. After Jackie made the drill team, the others would be eager to leave the Gray Area and go into the dazzling inner circle of the popular crowd.

"I'll practice tonight," she promised. "And be ready for Wednesday."

Instead of practicing that evening, Jackie decided to rearrange her room. Now that she was her own person, she ought to fix up her room to reflect her own tastes.

Sharon had the bed against one wall, between the two windows, the dresser along the opposite wall, and the vanity table in the corner. A dull, unimaginative arrangement.

Jackie pushed all the furniture to the center of the room. Grunting, she shoved the bed into the far corner at an angle, like a hammock. She tugged the dresser where the vanity had been and scooted the vanity table next to the closet.

Then she stood back to survey the results. The mirror over her vanity now reflected the window, which was like having an extra window. There was less floor space with the bed angled that way, but who needed to walk around? Now the room had her personal stamp. She would no longer feel like a boarder in Sharon's old room.

"Are you nervous?" Frieda asked Jackie as they accompanied her to the gym where the tryouts were being held.

"A little." Jackie tugged at her shorts. She could twirl her rifle six times without dropping it; the rest should be easy.

"Don't be," Carol said. "You'll do just fine."

Her confidence buoyed, Jackie left her cheering section and joined the other girls on the floor. Nobody seemed to know what they were doing. Miss Huff's whistle shrilled. At her command, the girls fell into a ragged formation. Jackie secured a highly visible place, second from the front in the far right column.

"Ready?" Miss Huff shouted, even though no one was. She gave another blast of her whistle. "March!"

Suddenly Jackie discovered she couldn't march. Something she had done with ease in first grade, something any child could do, she couldn't! Miss Huff's whistle scared her, causing her to start off on the wrong foot. Jackie was immediately out of step. Attempting to correct her pace, she hop-skipped, but that threw her rhythm off even more. While everyone else was marching with crisp military precision, Jackie was just jumping around.

Fweeet! Miss Huff blew her whistle so hard her eyes bugged. The columns halted, bumping into one another. "You," she pointed to Jackie. "What are you doing?"

"Marching?" Jackie replied in small voice.

"It looks more like a Mexican hat dance." The teacher made a sharp "cut" gesture.

Jackie stumbled past the judges seated on the bleachers, mortified. She had been cut before the first pass because she couldn't march! She didn't want to face her friends, but they crowded around her.

"That old Miss Huff is so unfair," Frieda pronounced. "She just wanted to make an example of someone so the others would get scared and mess up."

"She couldn't have picked a better example," Jackie said, close to tears. "I was awful."

"It could have happened to anyone," Paula said loyally.

But it happened to her, Jackie Howard, the Howard sister who was going to surpass her older sister's achievements.

Jackie could always tell when a letter from Sharon had arrived in the mail. At dinner, her parents analyzed each sentence to determine if their daughter was getting enough sleep or eating properly or keeping the right company. Sharon's slapdash letters home were totally scrutinized.

It didn't seem possible, but Sharon was receiving more attention now that she was gone than when she had been living at home.

When her parents weren't discussing Sharon's latest escapades in minute detail, they were silent, undoubtedly thinking about Sharon and what she was doing that very second. Jackie gamely tried to fill those silences with bright chatter, but it had no effect. Sharon had left a gaping hole no one could fill, especially not Jackie.

Jackie limped into the house after the disastrous tryouts and was shocked out of her own misery when she saw her mother crumpled in a chair, the pages of a letter littered around her like autumn leaves.

"Mama," she cried. "What's wrong?"

"She left the dorm!" her mother announced tragically.

"Who left? Sharon? Is she missing? Have you called the police?" Since her mother's tone conveyed the absolute worst, Jackie naturally assumed something terrible had happened to Sharon.

"No, she's not missing. She *left the dorm*! She and three other girls got an apartment in town somewhere."

"Is that all?" Sharon had just *moved*, hardly any reason to dial 911.

"Is that all?" Her mother's voice escalated into the dangerous range. "Do you know what this means? Sharon moved out of the dorm *one day* past the refund limit. If she had notified us a day earlier, we could have gotten a partial refund. Now we have to pay her dorm fees *and* rent on this apartment."

Jackie was delighted to see her mother's anger. This was like the old times when Sharon was always doing something to make her mother mad. "You could just kill her, right?"

"No," Mrs. Howard said in a complete reversal. "I'm worried sick about her. Where is this place? Is it in a good section of town? Who are those girls she's living with? What are they eating?"

"What does Sharon say about it?" She read Sharon's description of the apartment. " 'It's on the top floor of this neat old house. The landlady is real old but very sweet. We have one big room

31

with a double bed and two single beds and a bath down the hall. Don't worry about meals, Mom. There's a hot plate here, and we have the use of one shelf in Mrs. Hanover's refrigerator for cold stuff.' That doesn't sound too bad.''

"A hot plate! Sharon threw away a paid-up meal ticket for a hot plate and a shelf in a refrigerator! Those girls won't cook. They'll all starve, if they don't freeze to death first.''

That night, her parents called Sharon and learned that Sharon moved off campus because she hated her roommate and didn't like the dorm rules. A group of girls found an apartment in town that was incredibly cheap, mainly because it was nothing but a converted attic. No curtains, no rugs, no linens, and no privacy, from the way friends paraded in and out of their place any time of the day or night.

Despite Sharon's reassurance that she was not living in rat-infested squalor, her parents held an emergency summit meeting. No one asked Jackie about the tryouts. Considering her performance, she didn't know whether to be glad or angry.

The next day after school, Jackie could barely open the front door — it was barricaded by an enormous carton.

"What's that?" she asked her mother, who bustled into the living room with some towels.

"Things for Sharon." Mrs. Howard stuffed the towels into the carton.

Jackie could see the box was already packed with a quilt, wash cloths, towels, and the drapes from her old bedroom. "Hey! Those are mine! You took the curtains right off my window," she protested.

"It's not your room anymore," her mother said, sealing the box shut with heavy tape. "I'm getting new drapes for the spare room anyway, when I have time."

"You'd have time if you stopped fooling with Sharon," Jackie muttered, taking her books back to her bedroom. What else of hers was her mother donating to Sharon?

Another huge carton blocked the hall. This one was filled with mismatched pots and pans, odds and ends of flatware, and an old set of Melmac, decorated with a design of violets against a teal-blue background. Jackie used to play set-the-table with those dishes and pretend important company was coming for dinner. Now Sharon was getting them.

When Jackie went into the bathroom, she discovered a third, much smaller, box on the clothes hamper. Marked Sharon's Care Package, this box contained shampoo, soap, tissues, hand lotion, baby powder, and toilet paper. Her mother must have scoured the house the whole day, to collect three cartons' worth of stuff.

Mrs. Howard came into the hall to tape the pots-and-pans box.

"What are you going to do with these boxes?" Jackie asked her.

"Ship them. Sharon needs these things right away. We'd drive out there, but your father has to work this weekend."

"You're shipping *toilet paper*?" Jackie was incredulous. "All Sharon has to do is call and whine she doesn't have any toilet paper and you rush to send it to her! Can't she walk to the drug store and get some?"

"You know it's not just toilet paper," her mother said. "She doesn't have anything in that apartment."

"Whose fault is that? Who told her to move out? Why does everybody go off the deep end around here over every little thing Sharon does?"

Mrs. Howard stopped taping to stare at her. "What's wrong with you, Jackie?"

"I don't know." She did but she wasn't telling.

"Well, I'm sure I don't. It's no skin off your nose if we send some things to your sister. I don't know what's gotten into you lately." Her mother looked disappointed, as if she knew about the tryouts and how her second daughter had failed marching.

When Sharon left for college, Jackie thought *she'd* be the most important daughter. Oh, her parents paid attention to *her*, but not the way Jackie wanted.

It was like that time in sixth grade. Jackie couldn't grasp long division to save her life so her mother volunteered to help her. Every night for one hour they'd sit at the kitchen table and go over Jackie's arithmetic homework. Her mother would work a problem, then give Jackie a problem to work. Jackie understood the process only while her mother explained it. She thought she had long division licked at last, but the instant her mother assigned Jackie a problem to work on her own, Jackie couldn't remember how to begin. She'd write out the problem, drawing the long division symbol carefully, stalling for time, until her mother would say in exasperation, "Jackie, I just *showed* you how to do that."

"I can't do it," Jackie would whimper.

"You *can* do it. I'm not going to do it for you. Your teacher says you give up too easily. Try again."

But she couldn't do it unless her mother guided her through the procedure. It was her mother who gave up, unable to break through Jackie's mental block. Sharon took over helping Jackie with her homework. Sharon's method was to copy the answers from the back of the book and spend the rest of the hour joking and drawing funny pictures.

The *F* Jackie received on her long division test didn't hurt nearly as much as her mother's look of disappointment. The same look she gave Jackie now.

The feelings between her and her mother were almost like those long-ago evenings at the kitchen table, her mother patiently showing Jackie how to work a problem and Jackie nervously watching, knowing she wouldn't be able to do it when her turn came.

Even the cat knew Jackie was sadly deficient when it came to being the important Howard sister.

It wasn't dumb luck that caused her to flub the tryout. She simply wasn't good enough.

Chapter 4

Jackie was in her room with her math homework spread out on the floor, trying to ignore the fact that there were twenty-five tins of buttermints in the next room.

The buttermints were part of a fund-raiser her mother's women's club was sponsoring. Money from the sale of the candy would be donated to charity.

Right now Jackie could only think of one charity — herself. She loved buttermints. And dinner hadn't been that great, with only plain Jell-O for dessert. Plain because Jackie had eaten the frozen whipped topping earlier, then put the empty plastic tub back in the freezer so her mother wouldn't suspect.

Mrs. Howard discovered the empty container as she was dishing out the Jell-O. "Why do you leave empty boxes in the freezer?" she asked. "I've told you about that a thousand times. I thought with Sharon in college, I might be able to keep a few crumbs in the house for five minutes."

"All I did was eat the rest of the Cool Whip. I haven't been on a goodie raid since Sharon left," Jackie said in an injured tone, as if deprived of a vital part of her daily routine.

In a way, she was.

Sharon started the ritual of goodie raids. Whenever their parents left the house, the girls raided the cupboards for candy bars and cookies that their mother stashed in various places to put in their father's lunch. Once Mrs. Howard came back unexpectedly to find Jackie teetering on a chair, exploring the high shelves over the stove, while Sharon pilfered through the flour, tea, and coffee canisters.

"What are you doing?" their mother had demanded.

"Looking for goodies," Sharon replied, pertly. "You see, Mom, Jackie and I have a sugar deficiency. We just don't get enough."

"You get plenty," Mrs. Howard replied. "So this is what you girls do when your father and I turn our backs."

They did that and a lot of other things, like snooping in bureau drawers, trying on their mother's clothes, and reading important household papers that were none of their business. There was never a boring moment as long as Sharon was around.

Sharon had been gone over a month. Although Jackie resented the way her parents acted, she missed her sister. The missing moments came at odd times, like now, and hit her sharply, like a craving for sugar.

Abandoning her math homework, a lost cause anyway, Jackie surrendered to the Call of the Buttermint. She missed her sister so much right then, only a sweet, buttery mint melting slowly on her tongue could make her feel better.

The tins were stacked neatly beside the bed in Jackie's old room. Jackie picked up one tin and pried off the lid. The aroma of buttermints nearly overpowered her for a moment. She really *did* have a sugar deficiency. Paper dividers separated the pastel candies into four flavors. Jackie popped a pink mint into her mouth and let it melt until her whole system was flooded with delicious buttery sweetness. She sampled each flavor several times, with only a twinge of guilt. After all, there were lots of mints left in the tin and twenty-four whole other tins besides.

Jackie closed the box and placed it on the bottom of the pile, a ploy Sharon would have been proud of. But raiding wasn't any fun without Sharon. Nothing was, really. All the things she did with Sharon suddenly seemed unreal, as if she'd dreamed them.

Jackie wandered into her parents' room. Becoming her own person, she thought, was a lonely business.

Above her mother's bureau hung a plastic picture of a puppy, a dime store Mother's Day present from Sharon. The picture frame was in the shape of an arch, with a deep depression in the bottom for flowers. On one memorable goodie raid, Sharon unearthed a Snickers bar in her mother's dresser. She split the candy with Jackie, making sure she kept the biggest half for herself. After one bite, Sharon screeched, "Worms! Arrgghh! It's got worms!"

Jackie, who hadn't bit into her half yet, threw the candy bar down as if it burned her fingers. "Worms! Yuck! How do worms get in candy?"

"I don't know," Sharon gagged, "but I'm getting rid of mine this instant!" Standing on tiptoe, she stuffed the rest of her candy bar in the frame of the puppy picture. "I'll put yours in, too."

Because the picture was too high to be dusted regularly, the girls' secret went undetected for months. Checking the status of the Snickers bar became part of their snooping routine, the hidden wormy candy bar a Jackie-and-Sharon artifact.

Now Jackie was tall enough to reach the picture frame without having to be lifted up by her sister. She touched the fossilized candy, reassured. Sharon had been there. It wasn't a dream.

"Homecoming elections are rigged," Frieda stated one day at lunch. "The football team nominates the girl they want to win, along with a bunch of hopeless ones."

"I don't think so," Jackie contradicted. "My sister was nominated queen last year, and this other girl only beat her by a few votes."

40

"How awful," said Paula. "I bet she cried for weeks." She looked as if she might cry herself, just thinking about it.

Jackie shrugged. "She didn't mind. She'd been on the homecoming court when she was a sophomore. And she was queen of the sweetheart dance later that year." Sharon never lacked for titles or accolades.

"I've seen pictures of your sister in the yearbook archives," Carol said. "She's gorgeous. She has the prettiest hair."

It was the week before homecoming. The game and the dance that followed were the hottest topics of conversation in Fairfax High. All around her, in class, in the halls, in the cafeteria, Jackie heard other kids hatching plans about how they'd get to the game, what they'd wear to the dance, etc. Down the table from where they were eating lunch, a group of juniors debated which pizza parlors were the best to celebrate their victory over Washington-Lee.

Paula sighed. "I'll bring the munchies," she said wanly. "Popcorn, potato chips, stuff like that. What about soft drinks?"

"I'll get those," Carol said. "It'll be at my house so I should. And I'll ask my mom to make some brownies or something. Anything else you guys want?"

"A date for homecoming," Jackie murmured.

"You don't ask for much," Frieda said sourly. "Why not ask for something simple, like world peace?"

Not only were the four of them dateless, they

41

weren't even going to the game, which was why they were planning a slumber party at Carol's house.

At first the slumber party seemed like a good idea, but now Jackie wasn't so sure. She could imagine how it would go: they'd sprawl around in pajamas and bunny slippers, eating too much and complaining about how dumb it was to be a slave to tradition, and how the Rebels would probably lose anyway, and weren't they smart to stay home so they wouldn't have to live that down the rest of the year like those turkeys who went. It would undoubtedly be that way for every major event, the sweetheart dance, Sadie Hawkins, maybe right on through the junior ring dance and their senior prom.

Jackie didn't want to spend high school commiserating with her friends. She liked Frieda, but the girl's attitude irritated her. Frieda made being a freshman more of an ordeal than it was. She had evidently decided in the cradle that life was unfair, and she wouldn't give it half a chance.

"You know," Jackie began hesitantly. "We could go. Just to the game. Nobody needs a date for the game. I really hate to miss homecoming."

"So do I," Paula agreed instantly. "I feel like I've waited my whole life for this."

"Me, too," Carol put in.

Frieda was silent.

Jackie realized she had proposed more than just going to the homecoming game. It meant venturing beyond the security they had of anonymity and being noticed. Despite her spectacular failure at the drill team tryouts, Jackie still had high hopes for her freshman year.

"Let's do it," she said, this time with more conviction.

Carol cried, "Four girls at a football game. We might meet some boys!"

"Anything could happen." Jackie looked at Frieda. Frieda was the key. If the leader of their group endorsed the plan, then they would all feel braver. "Frieda? Are you with us?"

Frieda drew in a deep breath. "Jason will drive us. He doesn't know it yet, but he's going to take us. We'll meet at my house, okay? That way your parents will only have to pick you up. And we avoid the hassle of finding each other in that mob scene."

Plus there is safety in numbers, Jackie thought. None of them would have to face the new experience alone. Then she grinned at her friends. They were going to do it!

The phone rang. Jackie was positive it was Sharon. She'd been thinking about her sister so hard, wishing she would call, Sharon must have heard her! She ran to get the phone.

Sure enough, the voice on the other end said, "Hey, Bony Maronie! What's up?"

"Sharon!" Jackie blurted out, not even minding Sharon's old nickname. "I knew it was you! Did you get my letter? How come you never write to me? Guess what? I'm going to the homecoming game! When are you coming home? Are you coming home this weekend?"

"Gosh, Jackie, you wouldn't believe how busy I am. I hardly have time to breathe."

"Then you're not coming home this weekend?" Jackie had almost convinced herself that Sharon was packing that very minute.

"No. I can't come home till Thanksgiving. How's Felix? Do you kiss him every day like I told you?"

"When I can catch him. He doesn't like to be kissed. You know how your cat is." Jackie had so much to tell Sharon, about her new friends, their plans for homecoming, but her excitement dribbled away as she felt the miles, all one hundred of them, between her and her sister. Sharon was so far away.

"How come you never write to me? You promised you would," she accused.

"I know." Sharon sounded contrite. "Every time I write to Mom, I start to write to you, too, but it's always so late and I have so much studying to do."

"What's it like there?" Jackie asked.

Sharon didn't answer immediately. "It's — different. Not like home at all. Sometimes . . ."

"Sometimes what?"

She sighed. "Sometimes I feel kind of funny, being away. I miss everybody."

"You couldn't wait to go," Jackie pointed out.

"I know," Sharon agreed. "I'm glad I'm here . . . most of the time. Gosh, this is costing a mint. Is Mom around?"

Mrs. Howard had come in from the kitchen

and was motioning that she wanted to speak to Sharon.

"Right here," Jackie said. "Well . . . I guess I won't see you till Thanksgiving. Next time write to *me*. Bye." She loitered long enough to determine that Sharon really wanted an outfit she had forgotten and couldn't live without another day. Mrs. Howard promised to ship the outfit UPS. Jackie wondered if Sharon had called because she was lonely and used the clothes as an excuse.

Then she dismissed the idea. Sharon always had loads of friends. How could someone as popular as her sister ever be lonely?

Friday, the day of the homecoming game, a pep rally preempted sixth period. Jackie and her friends sat together in the bleachers. The band played rousing marches, every other one the school fight song. Jackie screamed until she was hoarse as their team, the Fairfax Rebels, sprinted out onto the field in their blue and gray uniforms. She couldn't wait until the game!

"Be at my house by six-thirty," Frieda said as they walked out to the buses. "Remember, we're all wearing jeans and sweaters." Frieda was acting as if going to the game was entirely her idea, but Jackie didn't care.

She climbed happily on her bus. It was a beautiful autumn afternoon. Just right for a football game. In a few hours, she and her friends would be attending their first important high school function.

At home, Jackie threw her books on the chair

by the door and ran into the kitchen to tell her mother she didn't want any supper, that she was too excited to eat.

Her mother wasn't in the kitchen. Through the window, Jackie could see her in the backyard, hanging up what looked like a bushel of laundry.

Whistling the school fight song, Jackie pranced back to her room to lay out the sweater and jeans she'd wear later that evening.

As she passed her old room, she noticed the door was partly open. Someone was moving around in there. A red-haired woman, rummaging through a suitcase. When Jackie uttered a sound of surprise, the woman turned and said, with a familiar grin, "Hi, Bony Maronie."

It was Sharon.

Chapter 5

"Sharon!" Jackie squealed. "What are you doing here? I thought you weren't coming this weekend."

"I changed my mind," Sharon replied. "Actually, some girls from Fairfax decided at the last minute to go home for homecoming and I hitched a ride. So here I am. Aren't you glad to see me? It feels so good to be home!"

"Sure I'm glad to see you! But what have you done to your hair?" Jackie had never seen hair that color before, a dark burgundy red, almost purple. "What did Mama say about it? I bet she was mad."

"Jackie, I'm my own person now. I like being a redhead. Anyway, at the beauty academy we're forever tinting our hair. It keeps us sane. Sit down and I'll tell you about my adventures."

47

"Do we have time before the game?" Jackie asked. "You are going, aren't you?"

"The girl I rode with is picking me up at seven. Plenty of time. I'll do your hair special for your big night, how's that?" She hauled an enormous tote bag from the corner. "I have to practice, you know. I plan to take my state boards in the spring. Go get a chair."

Jackie eagerly got her mother's sewing bench. Not only did she have her sister back but she was going to the game with a drop-dead hairstyle. When she was settled with a box of butterfly clips in her lap, Sharon began brushing her hair with hard professional strokes.

"Your hair's really growing," Sharon observed. "I bet it's long enough to put up."

"Don't do anything too fancy," Jackie cautioned her sister. "I don't want to look weird."

"You won't. You'll be gorgeous," Sharon promised. "You wouldn't believe the stuff I have to learn. Electricity, the bones in the human body, *chem*istry! All that to become a hairdresser. And the business courses at Madison . . . I'll be ready to take over General Motors by the time I'm finished."

"Don't you do permanents and facials and things like that?" Jackie asked.

"Bend your head." Sharon swirled Jackie's hair from the nape of the neck. "Okay, now hand me the clips, one at a time. Yeah, I went out on the floor last week. My first customer was a nightmare!"

"Really?" She handed Sharon a pink clip.

"I wouldn't lie. These two sisters come in — huge, both of them. They called each other 'Sissy.' One would say, 'Sissy, should I get it cut short or just have a trim?' and the other would say, 'Oh, Sissy, you'd look darling in short hair.' None of us could keep a straight face. Naturally, I got one of the sisters. She wanted a perm, a haircut, *and* a set."

Jackie winced as Sharon slid a sharp-pointed clip into the back of her ear. "That's a lot for your first job."

"I was so nervous it took me forever. I mean *all day*. I spent hours on that poor woman. The sisters kept passing each other notes under the dryers. I know they were complaining about me."

Jackie giggled. She could just picture the two ladies, their heads bristling with rollers, writing indignant notes on scraps torn from old magazines. Poor Sharon! "What'd you do?" She loved it that her sister was confiding in her.

"I just had to tough it out," Sharon replied. "When I was doing my customer's comb-out, I asked her how she wanted it, and she said, 'I don't care what you do to it, just get me out of here!' " She took two more clips from Jackie, then said, "Okay, you're done. How do you like it?"

Jackie turned to see herself in the mirror. Her whole head sprouted butterfly clips. Her hair, which she normally wore flowing past her shoulders, was now piled on top of her head in a complicated arrangement of curls and loops. She looked like Martha Washington.

"Well?" Sharon prompted, making a few more swipes at Jackie's towering hair. "What do you think?"

She had to handle this with tact. "I love it, but — well, isn't it a little too much for a football game?" Actually, the hairstyle would have been too much for the inaugural ball. At her sister's expression of dismay, Jackie hastily added, "I mean, I don't want to show up my friends. Next to me, they'll just be . . . ordinary." She nearly said "normal."

Sharon studied her with a critical frown. "You know what's wrong? Your face is too small for all this hair. You need your eyebrows plucked. That'll open up your eyes, make them look bigger." She began rooting in her tote bag for tweezers.

"No, wait — "

"Close your eyes," Sharon ordered. "Don't flinch. I'll pull each hair in the direction it's growing. It won't hurt a bit."

Either Sharon's sense of direction was off or the tweezers were dull because Jackie couldn't remember when she'd been in such agony. As Sharon wrenched each hair, tears of pain streamed from Jackie's eyes, and she sneezed violently after each extraction.

Sharon mumbled something about having to remove a couple more to "even them up." At last she put the tweezers down. "Don't look yet.

I have to get my eyebrow pencil."

Jackie's eyes flew open. The image that stared back at her in the mirror looked surprised. No wonder. She had no eyebrows left. *None.* "Sharon!" she screamed. "I don't have any eyebrows!" She burst into tears.

"It's not as bad as it looks," Sharon said hastily. "Don't get upset. I'll lend you my eyebrow pencil until your eyebrows grow back in. I'm really sorry, Jackie. I kept trying to even them up and — well . . . I'm still new at this."

"You ruined me! I can't go to the game like this. Can't you cut off little pieces of hair and glue them on or something?"

"No." Sharon bit her lip. "I'm sorry," she said again. "Here, let me draw you some new eyebrows."

When Sharon finished, Jackie forced herself to look in the mirror. The result was far from perfect, in her opinion. Sharon had drawn arched brows that made Jackie appear to have a perpetual sneer. Now she looked like Martha Washington smelling something bad.

How could Sharon do this to her? They had been getting along so well, really talking, and Sharon had to go and ruin the good close feeling. Sharon had been home less than an hour and already she'd turned Jackie's life upside-down. Sharon hasn't lost her touch, Jackie thought.

The bleachers were packed. Jackie and her friends had to sit in two different rows, but they were still together.

"Everybody will think you're going to the dance afterward, with that hairstyle," Frieda told Jackie. "We're jealous."

"Don't be," Jackie said, pulling her hair down to cover her weird drawn-on eyebrows. "I feel like a radio antenna with all these clips sticking out."

"Is she here?" Paula asked from the seat below Jackie.

"Somewhere. She came with a bunch of old grads." Jackie scanned the bleachers but couldn't spot her sister.

The band poured out onto the field, followed by the drill team and high-stepping majorettes. Floats from each class circled the football field. The homecoming court waved from the last float. Jackie began to respond to the excitement of the evening. She felt proud to be part of wonderful traditions like homecoming.

At least, she did until the announcer asked the former graduates to rise so they could be acknowledged. On the other side of the bleachers, where the rival team's supporters were seated, a group of girls stood and waved wildly. Jackie recognized Sharon's purply-red hair instantly. To her horror, her sister vaulted over the people in front of her to the ground below where the football team was benched. Amid claps and catcalls, Sharon planted a kiss on the captain's football helmet. He quickly ripped off his helmet to collect another kiss, this time on the lips. Other boys reached down to help

Sharon back up into the stands. Everyone in the entire stadium was laughing.

Everyone except Jackie, who was shriveling with embarrassment.

"Was that your sister?" Frieda said with awe. Jackie nodded, too humiliated to speak.

People joked about the kissing bandit throughout the game. A black cloud of jealousy descended over Jackie, dampening her enthusiasm. Why couldn't Sharon have been content to stand up with the rest of the returning graduates, wave, and sit down without making a scene? Did she always have to be the star?

Jackie watched the game without following a single play. Only when people began filing out of the bleachers did she realize their team had lost to Washington-Lee, fourteen to nine. The kiss from the mysterious red-haired girl hadn't been such good luck after all.

Jackie got home from the game before Sharon and was in bed staring at a book, but actually contemplating various slow methods of murder, when her sister barged into her room.

"Don't you ever knock?" Jackie demanded.

"You never knocked on my door when I was home." Sharon nearly fell over the vanity table. "What's this doing here?"

"I put it there."

Sharon glanced around the room. "What have you done to my room? It looks like a warehouse."

"It does not. Anyway, it's *my* room."

Sharon plopped on the bed with Jackie. "Good grief! How do you keep from getting dizzy with the bed at this angle?"

"Nobody asked you in here," Jackie said primly, edging away from her sister. "And nobody asked your opinion about where I put my bed." Truthfully, Jackie wasn't crazy with the new arrangement of her room. She was forever bumping into the vanity when she got up in the night to go to the bathroom. Sometimes when she woke up, she didn't know where she was.

"This is just like old times, you and me talking at night. How'd you like the game?" Sharon asked. "Wasn't it great?"

"We lost. How great could it be if we lost?" Jackie knew Sharon was alluding to the kissing incident. Her sister had received flattery and attention the entire evening — she didn't need it from Jackie. And Jackie wasn't about to give it to her.

"The homecoming queen was pretty, wasn't she?" Jackie goaded.

"Marybeth Wellington? I guess she was the best they could do. I mean, the prettiest girls graduated last year. Did you see the drill team? They were all over the field. Half of them couldn't twirl worth beans."

"At least they could march," Jackie said, realizing too late she hadn't told Sharon about trying out.

"Of course they could march. *Any*one can march." Sharon poked her. "Don't tell me — "

54

"I tried out," Jackie blurted. "Miss Huff cut me in the first round."

"You couldn't march?" Sharon said unbelievingly.

"I started off on the wrong foot. It could happen to anyone," Jackie explained, furious. "You don't know. You weren't there. Even if you were, you wouldn't have paid attention to me. You're always too busy stealing the limelight."

"Don't blame me for your two left feet. And I do not steal the limelight. It just sort of follows me." Sharon rose on one elbow. "Besides, I'm responsible for your stage debut, remember?"

How could she forget?

Sharon's fourth-grade class had put on a play for the PTA. Jackie, who wasn't in school yet, went with her parents. When the play was over, Sharon piped to her teacher, "My little sister can sing! Want to hear her?" Sharon's teacher looked skeptical, but gave her consent.

Sharon prodded Jackie up on the stage. "Sing the song I taught you," she hissed.

Excited by all the attention, but numb with stage fright, Jackie stood frozen until Sharon swatted her. "Sing!"

Barely moving her lips and in a voice so low it couldn't be heard in the first row, Jackie sang, "Little Tommy Tinker, sat on a clinker and he began to cry. Ma-ma, ma-ma, what a poor boy am I!"

The kids in Sharon's class laughed, and Sharon's teacher pronounced the performance very nice, but Jackie noticed people leaving the auditorium.

"Some stage debut," Jackie remarked acidly. "Everybody walked out."

"They couldn't hear you. You know, Jackie, some people don't shine in the limelight."

Jackie flapped the covers. "Get out of my bed! I'm trying to go to sleep."

"Boy, are you grumpy," Sharon said, climbing off of Jackie's bed.

"It's a scientific fact that people without eyebrows are grouchy."

"I told you I was sorry. And they'll grow back," Sharon said, going to the door. She sang, very softly, "Ma-ma, ma-ma, what a poor boy am I!"

Jackie seethed with anger. Her sister was such a creep, rubbing in Jackie's failures. After her glorious moment at the game, Sharon was pretty full of herself.

Jackie stared at the ceiling a few minutes, then she got up and began moving her furniture back to the way it had been originally.

"This is the last of it." Jackie plunked the laundry basket on the floor in the spare room.

Sharon lay on the rumpled bed, studying a textbook. Felix was stretched out beside her. Every microinch of the guest room was occupied by Sharon's clothes, which were stacked on the floor, the dresser, and the bed.

"You can say thank you," Jackie said.

"Thank you," Sharon parroted, without lowering her book.

The whole weekend had been a disaster. Sharon ate, slept, talked on the phone, and ordered Jackie around like a galley slave. On top of that, Jackie had to help her mother with Sharon's laundry. And the ingrate couldn't even be bothered to say thanks!

"When are you going back to Harrisonburg?" Jackie asked. Any time within the next twenty seconds or so would be all right with her.

"Donna's coming by at six." Sharon put her book down and sat up, yawning. "I'll be glad, too. It was nice to be home but kind of strange to be in the guest room. And there isn't anything to *do* here."

"You managed to keep busy eating," Jackie said, rather nastily.

"Only because Mom kept dangling seven-course meals in front of me. I had to eat what she cooked, didn't I?"

"Yes, but you didn't have to put in requests. Fried chicken for breakfast? Really, Sharon."

"Well, she asked me what I wanted and I told her." Sharon yawned again.

"Be careful when you get out of bed," Jackie warned. "You don't want to faint when all the blood rushes to your head."

"I haven't been lying around that much."

"You have permanent marks from the bedspread on your body."

Jackie went out to the kitchen. Her mother

was packing a carton with groceries. "It's too early for the Thanksgiving canned drive," she said, knowing full well the care package was for Sharon.

Mrs. Howard tucked a can opener into the box. "Those girls don't eat. They live on peanut butter crackers and soft drinks. Did you see how Sharon ate this weekend? She's starving. Her stomach's shrunk up to nothing."

Anyone who could down chicken, five biscuits with honey, and a platter of fried potatoes for *breakfast* hardly had a wizened stomach, but Jackie didn't comment.

At six o'clock, Sharon emerged from her room, wearing one of her freshly pressed outfits. Feeling like a bellhop, Jackie lugged three bulging duffel bags out to Sharon's ride's car. Jackie would have offered to walk behind the car and carry them herself, anything to get rid of Sharon.

After a tearful exchange of kisses and good-byes on the porch, Sharon got in the car. "See you at Thanksgiving!"

Jackie stood on the porch with her parents, who waved until the car was a dwindling dot.

As they went back into the house, Mrs. Howard said, "Jackie, would you please bring me Sharon's sheets?"

"Not more laundry!"

"Please," said Mrs. Howard. "No argument."

The guest room was a shambles. Jackie yanked the bedspread, kicking an object with her shoe. It was one of Sharon's socks, balled up and forgotten under the bed.

Jackie tossed the sock on the pile of sheets. Her mother would probably lovingly starch and iron the sock, then send it to Sharon, air-mail, special delivery.

The stripped bed looked forlorn. In fact, the room without Sharon made Jackie feel empty. If she was glad to see her sister leave, then how could she miss her already? But she did.

Then she realized she hadn't really hated having Sharon home. Sure, she was jealous of the way Sharon had been more pampered than Cleopatra, and she hated the fight they had had Friday night after the game. It set the tone for the whole weekend. And it was so dumb, arguing over who was hogging the limelight.

Two sisters who had a friendship pact should not act like two-year-olds. But maybe, Jackie thought, this was the way it would be between them from now on.

Chapter 6

Scritch, scritch, scritch. Paint chips flew as Jackie wielded the paint scraper in both hands. She stopped and stood back to see how much she had done and how much farther she had to go. The board stretched on for miles. Jackie had only scratched a six-inch section.

"This is going to take all night," she complained. "My wrists are killing me."

"So are mine," Mrs. Howard agreed amiably. She stood on a stepladder a little way down the patio, scraping the board above Jackie's. "You only have to do one board. I have five. And you're a lot younger than I am."

This wasn't the sympathetic answer Jackie wanted to hear. Instead of feeling sorry for her and letting her go back in the house to watch TV, her mother managed to make Jackie feel she should offer to scrape two boards, so her poor aged mother would only have to do four.

The afternoon sun beat against Jackie's neck as she resumed scraping. She'd put her long hair in a ponytail and was wearing cut-offs and a T-shirt, but she was still roasting. Indian summer, her father called it, getting that let's-paint-the-siding-while-the-weather-holds gleam in his eye. Jackie wasn't too surprised when her mother greeted her after school with her very own paint scraper.

She tried peeling the paint in one long strip, like paring a carrot, but the paint clung stubbornly to the siding, coming off in fitful patches and causing Jackie's scraper to skip and buckle like a bronco.

"Mama, this paint does not want to come off." She licked her knuckles. The skin on the back of her hand, she discovered ruefully, peeled more readily than old paint. "I don't know why Daddy wants to paint the house. It looks fine to me. At least, it did until we messed it up."

"This side of the house hasn't been touched for years. It really needs it," Mrs. Howard said, scraping industriously. A little blizzard of paint chips drifted around the base of her ladder. "You're making it worse by resting every two seconds. Put a little elbow grease in it, Jackie. I want to get done before supper."

Jackie rasped away at a miniscule portion, wondering how many other fourteen-year-olds had to work as hard as she did in order to get a bit of supper. Certainly not Sharon. When

Sharon was her age, she didn't even get up to switch her own TV channel. She always asked Jackie to do it. Jackie the Slave.

Jackie tipped her head back to gaze at the red-gold leaves against the blue sky, a view infinitely prettier than the half-scraped board in front of her. A buttermint would taste good right about now. She couldn't very well put her scraper down and tell her mother she was going in to steal some more mints that were supposed to be sold for charity. But she *could* say she had to go to the bathroom. Even slaves were entitled to a break. She'd sneak into the guest room instead and gobble a handful of mints —

"Jackie!" her mother's voice cut sharply into her thoughts. "Stop daydreaming and get busy."

"I'm not daydreaming," Jackie said defensively. "I was thinking about Sharon."

"What about her?"

"Well, when she was my age, she didn't have to do a thing. All she did was back the car up and down the driveway and play the radio." Remembering her sister's soft life made Jackie resolve to take *two* handfuls of buttermints.

"No, she didn't either," her mother contradicted, moving the ladder. "She only drove the car a few times. Your father wouldn't let her every time she asked."

"Still," Jackie said, hoping to drag the argument out to the point where her mother would become exasperated and send her indoors. "She was driving when she was only fourteen. A whole year before she had behind-the-wheel driver's training.''

In one of those weird flashback moments she'd been experiencing since Sharon left for college, Jackie was suddenly ten years old again, sitting in the passenger seat while Sharon slowly backed the car all the way down the steep driveway, almost to the road, then drove too fast up the hill, gunning the engine so gravel spun beneath the tires. Mr. Howard watched from a lawn chair. On every pass, he pointed out Sharon's mistakes.

It was a strange way to spend an afternoon, going up and down the driveway. At the time, Jackie never realized they weren't going anywhere, because Sharon made the trip seem real. Her sister draped her arm out the window, just like their father did, and kept looking in the mirrors as if she were actually on the highway. Over the blare of the radio, Sharon described the scenery. One time, they'd be heading for Ocean City. Another, they were driving into Washington, D.C.

Jackie enjoyed playing Sharon's passenger. She sat with her sister's purse in her lap, looking through the pictures in Sharon's wallet. Tucked beside a snapshot of her current boyfriend was a corner torn off a twenty dollar bill, a souvenir of one of their dates. Jackie was awestruck. She knew you weren't supposed to deface money — it was against the law. Only her confident sister would have the nerve to ask her date to rip the corner of his twenty dollar bill before paying their bill.

That was what burned in her memory — riding up and down the driveway on a bright Indian summer day like this one, staring at the corner of a twenty dollar bill in her sister's wallet.

"Sharon had it easy," Jackie said. "I don't notice anyone tossing *me* the car keys."

"You and Sharon are entirely different," her mother pointed out. "Sharon was ready to drive at fourteen. She would have driven at twelve if we would have let her. To my knowledge, you've never mentioned wanting to learn until this instant." She glanced over at Jackie, wary. "And I bet you brought it up now just to start an argument."

Her mother had come perilously close to the truth. In order to throw her off the scent, Jackie said, with genuine resentment, "Sharon got to do everything she wanted because she's the oldest, and you like her the best. You only had me so I could scrape paint and work in the garden, isn't that right?"

"That's nonsense and you know it."

"Is it? What about the baby book and the baby shoes?" She scraped a long line of paint, gouging the tool into the wood. "You saved all those things when Sharon was a baby, but after I came along, you were bored with the whole idea."

Mrs. Howard sighed. "If you mention that baby-book business one more time — "

"The proof's in your bottom drawer, Mama,"

Jackie accused. "I could go get them right now and show you — "

"Keep scraping," her mother ordered. "I know exactly where the baby books are."

Jackie had discovered the great baby-book discrepancy when she was in first grade. A boy in her class brought his baby book in to Show and Tell. When Jackie got home that day, she asked Sharon if they had baby books. With a smug little smile, Sharon took Jackie into their mother's room and opened the bottom drawer of her bureau. She pulled out two books, one as big as a kite, covered in padded satin with ribbons and roses and "Our Baby" in fancy writing; the other a puny *paperback* with a coffee stain on the dog-eared cover.

Sharon's book, the beautiful one, of course, was filled with photos of a basketball-headed baby and lavish descriptions of her first tooth, her first word (which Jackie thought should have been "me" but was actually "mama"), her first step, etc.

Someone had dutifully recorded Jackie's birth statistics on the first page of her book, but that was all before the person decided to use the book as a coaster. The rest of the book, such as it was, contained only blank pages. According to Jackie's baby book, she never got a first tooth, took her first step, or uttered her first word.

Then there was the matter of the baby shoes. Sharon's first tiny slippers had been bronzed into an ashtray. No one ever used the ashtray but it sat on the television set in the place of honor. Sharon's walking shoes, tie shoes sturdier than the dainty slippers, had been bronzed into bookends. Jackie couldn't go through the living room, it seemed, without bumping into a piece of Sharon's clothing that had been immortalized in bronze.

And where were Jackie's baby shoes? In the bottom drawer of her mother's dresser, unbronzed and forgotten.

"How come you never had my shoes made into an ashtray?" Jackie asked now. "How come you never wrote in my baby book? Where'd you get that crummy old baby book anyhow? Did they give those away at the supermarket or what?"

"Jackie, why do you worry me with silly things?" Her mother shifted the ladder once more. She had scraped two boards and Jackie wasn't a third finished with her one board.

"It's not silly. You won't admit you love Sharon the most, even when the proof is in your dresser." Anger over the inequality between them spurred Jackie into scraping harder than ever.

"I've told you a dozen times, somebody gave me that fancy book at my baby shower. I never could have afforded anything so expensive." Mrs. Howard paused to brush paint chips from the bandanna that covered her hair. "I don't remember where I got your baby book."

"Probably from Safeway," Jackie muttered.

"I did not. The reason I didn't write much in yours was because Sharon was into everything and I didn't have time."

"See? Sharon comes first. She always has and she always" — with a final surge of energy, Jackie came to the end of her board — "will!"

Her mother climbed down the ladder. "What is wrong with you, Jackie? Are you having problems at school?"

"No," Jackie cried. "I have problems at home!" Flinging her scraper into the yard, she ran into the house. She heard her mother calling her, but she didn't stop until she was locked in her old bedroom.

Her mother came to the door and tried the knob. "Jackie, are you okay? Open the door and we'll talk."

"I'm okay. I just want to be alone," she replied.

Huddled at the foot of the bed, she gobbled buttermints from four different tins. She reached up and switched on the radio. An instrumental song was playing. She recognized drooling clarinet notes. Jackie hated clarinet music because it always reminded her of someplace she had been once but couldn't get back to. She didn't understand why she felt that way since she'd never really been anywhere.

After supper, a hurried affair of hot dogs, leftover mashed potatoes, and canned black-eyed peas, Jackie went into her room.

Her mother followed her. "Jackie, are you busy with your homework?"

"No." Her school books were still in the chair.

Mrs. Howard sat on the bed. "I want to talk to you. You seem very unhappy lately. What is bothering you?"

"Nothing." She felt all jangly inside, and a little sick, but was unwilling to talk about it.

Her mother fingered a hole Felix had gnawed in the dust ruffle. "You miss Sharon, don't you?"

"Why should I miss the Queen of the Universe? She wasn't home five minutes and she plucked out all my eyebrows and made me go to homecoming looking like Martha Washington."

Mrs. Howard tried to hide her smile, but wasn't quick enough.

"It's not funny, Mama," Jackie said. "How would you like to draw on half your face every single day? And I never get them to match."

"Sharon said she was sorry. And they're growing back. Your sister has to practice. She can only learn by doing."

"Well, let her learn on somebody else. I'm tired of being Sharon's guinea pig."

"Is that all that's bothering you?" her mother pressed.

Felix wandered into the room. He knocked his hard head at Jackie's ankles. She stroked his shiny black fur. "The kids at school keep teasing me," she said.

"About your eyebrows?"

"No. About Sharon. You know that crazy stunt she pulled at the game, kissing the captain of the football team? They keep calling me Sharon Howard's little sister."

"Well, you are, aren't you?"

"That's not the *point*," she exclaimed. "The point is, that's who they know me as — Sharon's little sister. I don't *want* to be Sharon's little sister. I want to be . . . my own self."

"You are," her mother said. "This thing with Sharon will blow over soon — something else will come along for people to talk about. And as for wanting to be your own self, as you put it, I guess you have to let people *know* who you are."

Jackie stopped petting the cat and looked up at her mother. "You mean, I have to do things to make people notice me, like Sharon does?"

"I wouldn't go that far," her mother said wryly. "But that's the general idea. Only *you* know what kind of person you want to be, Jackie." She paused. "Is there anything else you'd like to tell me?"

She couldn't put it off any longer. Meeting her mother's eyes, she said, "Yes. I sort of . . . ate your buttermints."

"Ahhh. I've been waiting for your confession. Especially after I went into the spare room this evening to gather up the tins I sold and am supposed to deliver tomorrow."

Jackie could imagine what happened. Her mother probably picked up a tin, expecting it to be medium-heavy, then nearly dropped it, surprised at its lightness. Opening it, she would have seen there were only a few lone buttermints rattling around the bottom. All the tins were the same.

"How did you manage to eat twenty-five tins of buttermints?" her mother asked.

"I didn't do it all at once," Jackie said. "I started a few weeks ago. At first I only stole from one tin, but then that one got too low, so I added mints from the other tins, and then *those* tins got too empty because I couldn't stop eating them. . . ." Her voice died away. "Sharon ate some, too, when she was here," she added, rallying a little.

Her mother looked dubious. "Surely not as many as you did."

"No." Then, faintly, as if all the candy she'd eaten in the past weeks formed a huge lump in her stomach, "What are you going to do about the candy you sold?"

"I'll borrow from a lady in the club who hasn't sold her share," her mother replied. "And I will dock your allowance for the cost of the buttermints. If you would care to add more, our women's club would appreciate it." She got up and left.

It was really Sharon's fault that she ate the buttermints. Jackie was either mad at her sister or she missed her, but the cure was the same, a handful of buttermints. Her mother should demand the money from Sharon.

Jackie was supposed to go to the movies with Frieda and Carol and Paula that weekend. Now she couldn't go. When they asked her what happened to her allowance, she could always say she had given it to charity.

Chapter 7

When Carol Lewis, who was on the yearbook staff, told Jackie that yearbook photographers were going to be taking shots of the campus during lunch, Jackie decided to buy an apple and a carton of milk and eat outside that day. It was quite cool, too chilly, really, to sit on the front steps for forty-five minutes.

Maybe the cold will work in my favor — no competition, Jackie thought as she arranged herself on the shallow steps in a classic student pose, books scattered artfully beside her, the thickest opened across her knees, the straw in her milk carton bent just so.

She took a single bite out of the apple, then pretended to be totally absorbed in her studies while the three yearbook photographers set up their tripods.

Even though it was months away, Jackie was already anticipating the day the yearbooks were distributed. She couldn't wait to sniff the inky smell, crack the leather spine, feel the glossy pages. More than anything, she wanted to flip through her copy of the *FareFac Sampler*, past the sports photos, the shots of the cheerleaders, past the Computer and Math Club photos where the eggheads grinned stiffly, to the coveted candid pictures. Here, snapped for all eternity, was a progression of the little events that summarized the school year.

Jackie wanted to be surprised by her own face on those pages, a typical freshman student, yet special enough to be chosen as a representative of her class. She wanted her friends to exclaim, "Jackie! That's you!"

The closest she had come to being in a candid picture was the year before, but it was hardly anything to brag about. The pictures chronicling the eighth-grade class consisted mainly of staged shots: a phony food fight in the cafeteria, Cheryl Denton peering over a stall in the girls' room, Lucy Delmonico reading a book, held upside-down, naturally. On the next to last page was Jackie's arm.

She had been walking by when a photographer captured the moment when some girls finished braiding Maryann Long's hair into ridiculous pigtails. The photo had been cropped so that just Jackie's arm showed. Only Jackie knew it was her arm. None of her friends recognized her arm, even after she laid her real arm on the page for comparison.

Sharon was always included in two or three candid yearbook pictures, and not just her arm, either. It was time, Jackie decided, the rest of *her* was recorded for posterity.

The cement steps were uncomfortable. She stared hard in the direction of the photographers, who had quit fooling with light meters and were adjusting their cameras. Didn't they see a perfect shot when it was right in front of them?

At last they began snapping pictures. Jackie took another tiny bite of her apple. She was hungry enough to gobble the whole thing, but knew the apple was a central part of the composition of her picture.

"Hey, girl," one of the boys called.

Jackie pointed to herself. "Me?" she asked casually. Finally, someone realized he had the yearbook cover in his viewfinder.

"Yeah, you. Move to the right."

She shifted a few inches to the right, draping her skirt attractively, then smiled.

"More," the boy ordered. "Move over more."

"More?" Jackie scooted over about two feet. "How's this?"

He sighted through his viewfinder, then yelled, "No! Move way over. You're still in the picture."

In a huff, Jackie gathered her books and milk carton. Her hands full, she stuck the apple in her mouth and headed for the door. She'd starved herself and frozen to death, just to be told to get out of the picture!

Behind her, the photographers began snickering.

"Hey," the boy said again. "Look at me!"

Jackie turned as he clicked the shutter. Too late, she let the apple drop out of her mouth.

"You didn't take that!" she cried, horrified. "Will that be in the yearbook?"

"Don't worry," the boy said, advancing the film in his camera. "It probably won't turn out."

"I hope not."

Jackie forgot about the photo until the Wednesday before Thanksgiving.

Frieda stopped her in the hall. "Have you seen the school paper?"

"Not yet," Jackie replied. "I haven't been to homeroom yet. Why? What's in it?"

For an answer, Frieda showed her the latest issue of the *Rebel Yell*. On the front page, big as life, was the picture of Jackie with the apple in her mouth, like a suckling pig. The caption beneath read, "Can't wait till Thanksgiving."

Jackie groaned. This devastating picture was a hundred times worse than being an anonymous arm. "How could they do this to me? Do you suppose anyone will know it's me?"

"I did," Frieda said, not helping. She stared at the photograph, reconsidering. "With that apple covering half your face and your cheeks puffed out like that, maybe nobody will know it's you." She was wrong.

All that day people commented on the photograph. Boys made unflattering oink-oink noises when they saw her. Jackie was so embarrassed she could have died. She wanted to get out of the Gray Area of anonymity, but not this way!

When the last bell rang, she walked out to the buses with Frieda and Paula and Carol, her head down so she wouldn't be recognized.

"I think that black-haired lady is honking at you," Paula said.

Jackie looked up. "It's Sharon!" she gasped. "She's home from college." Dashing across the lawn, she called back, "Talk to you guys over the weekend. Bye!"

"You're home early," Jackie said as soon as she got in the car. "Mama wasn't expecting you till tonight. And you dyed your hair again!" Her sister seemed years older with jet-black hair and heavy eyeshadow.

Sharon roared out of the parking lot. "I thought I'd be a mysterious brunette this week."

"How's school?" Jackie asked, anxious to catch up on all the news. "Are you dating anybody?"

Sharon fluffed her black bangs. "School is fine. Busy. Some days I hardly know if I'm coming or going. Especially shuttling back and forth between the beauty academy and the college. But," she added with a sly smile, "I manage to find time for a handsome prelaw student."

"Is it serious?" Jackie pumped. Sharon flitted from boyfriend to boyfriend in high school, but always claimed she'd settle down once she got to college.

"I don't know," Sharon admitted. "We don't have that much time together. Hey, tell me what you've been up to." She pulled the car into their driveway.

"Well, this for starters." Jackie shook open a copy of the school newspaper under her sister's nose. "That's me on the front page."

Sharon stared at the photograph, then burst out laughing. "You look awful! Next time you have your picture taken, take the apple out of your mouth!"

"It was supposed to be funny," Jackie fibbed. "We did it like that on purpose." She crammed the paper back in her notebook, miffed. Why couldn't Sharon see that this picture set Jackie apart from the other ninth-graders? Not necessarily the recognition that Jackie had *wanted*, but recognition just the same.

The subject of the picture came up again during supper that evening. "What do you think of Jackie getting into the school newspaper?" Mr. Howard asked Sharon.

Sharon took the plate her mother handed her. "Good grief, Mom. Did you load this with a bulldozer?" Then she answered her father's question. "It's just the sort of stunt I'd do."

Mrs. Howard nodded. "I said that very same thing when Jackie showed us the picture. In fact, at first glance, it even looks like you."

Jackie was tired of listening to herself being discussed as if she weren't there. She jumped up, indignant. "It is *not* the sort of thing Sharon would do. *I* did it. Me! Not her!"

"Sit down, Jackie," her father said. "I don't know why we can't ever have a meal in this house without somebody acting dramatic."

"We know *you* did it," Mrs. Howard said. "That's your picture in the newspaper. It's just that it reminds us of the crazy tricks Sharon used to pull, that's all. Eat your dinner."

Jackie ate, but she wasn't happy. She was sick of being compared to Sharon. Even if she did hate the photograph, it was *hers*, something she had done on her own. But it wasn't hers any more. If Sharon hadn't already done it, then it was the sort of thing Sharon *would* do. That left no room for Jackie to initiate a single original act. She might as well give up.

The pattern for Sharon's visit home seemed set in concrete. Sharon slept late, but was rewarded with an enormous breakfast around the time Jackie was slapping together a peanut butter sandwich for lunch. She talked incessantly on the phone to her old friends, when she wasn't lounging in front of the television set.

"How come Sharon doesn't have to lift a finger around here?" Jackie whined as she helped her mother with the mountain of dishes from their Thanksgiving dinner.

"Sharon works very hard in school." Her mother propped the roasting pan to drain. "I'm worried about her. She's too thin and she's got circles under her eyes."

"That's eye makeup," Jackie said. But her point was already lost. Sharon slept enough for

78

two people, yet Mrs. Howard only saw the poor little match girl.

"It's not just her appearance. I'll always worry about Sharon. She jumps into things too fast."

"What things?" Jackie asked. She had never known her sister to jump into anything, unless you counted the time she fell through the living room ceiling in a friend's house.

"Sharon races through life at a breakneck speed," Mrs. Howard replied. "She doesn't slow down for curves."

"If she didn't, she wouldn't have got her driver's license."

Her mother smiled. "I mean she's impulsive. She does things without thinking."

"I'm like that, too," Jackie said, wanting her mother to worry about *her* getting hurt going around curves. "I just popped that apple in my mouth and the next thing I knew I was in the paper. People at school call me crazy now." They called her Miss Piggy, too, but she chose not to mention it.

"Well, I wouldn't put you quite in the same category as Sharon. I've had to keep my eye on her since she crawled out of the playpen. I could always trust you."

Of course. According to Sharon, Jackie had been a sappy baby, content to stay in the crib until she was twenty-seven months, and an even dopier toddler, who would color placidly until she was practically comatose and the crayons were worn down to stumps.

Jackie wiped the turkey platter. "I wish she'd

go back to school. I'm tired of being her slave."

"It's only for a few more days," her mother said. "You ought to spend some time with your sister."

"I wait on her enough, thank you." Jackie clambered up on a stool to put the platter away. She'd been so anxious for her sister to come home, hoping they'd have fun and make up for the disastrous homecoming weekend. But who wanted to spend time with a Sharon the Dictator?

Her mother sprinkled cleanser in the sink and began scrubbing. "She wants the car tomorrow. I'll give you two money so you can eat out. How's that?"

"Okay, I guess," Jackie said slowly. Going out to lunch with her sister sounded sort of fun. Maybe once they were away from their parents, they would talk, *really* talk, the way they used to.

When Sharon heard about the plan, she wasn't thrilled over the prospect of an outing with her little sister.

"Mom, I was going to see my old friends." After days of suspended animation, Sharon had finally roused herself. "I haven't seen anybody but family since I got home."

"You can take Jackie," her mother persisted. She handed Sharon ten dollars. "Treat yourselves to lunch."

As they drove down Lee Highway, heading toward Fairfax, Jackie said icily, "I'll sit in the car while you visit your friends." Sharon had made it clear she didn't want Jackie tagging along.

"I've changed my mind," Sharon said. "I'm not going to see them."

"Why? Because Mama made you take me along?"

"No. I just don't feel like it." She sighed. "I don't have much in common with them anymore. Linda works and all she talks about is her boring job. And Pat's getting married in the spring and that's all *she* talks about. It's funny, we were such good friends and now . . . it's sort of like coming back home. Nothing is really the same. Once you leave high school, everything changes."

Jackie was barely *in* high school, waiting for things to change. For the better.

"I'm hungry," said Sharon. "Let's go to Tops."

"Tops! Mama will kill you if she finds out you took me there." Jackie wasn't allowed to go to the teenage hang-out at the Circle.

"The only way she'll find out is if you blab. Well?" The question was a challenge.

"Sure." Maybe it was time to be a little reckless. After they got home and her mother asked where they had eaten, Jackie would smile and say, "Oh, just someplace."

Tops was the last drive-in restaurant in town that employed carhops. Sharon pulled in under the big red roof, beside a vacant speaker. They ordered hamburgers with the works, fries, and milkshakes. Jackie felt like a character in an old beach party movie.

The parking lot teemed with teenagers.

Sharon nudged Jackie. "Change places with me."

"Why?"

"Why do you always ask why? Just do it. Climb over me."

When they had switched places, Sharon cranked the window down, even though it was freezing outside. Jackie looked past her sister to see the reason for Sharon's sudden move. Two cute guys, both about Sharon's age, grinned at them from the next car.

Well! Jackie thought. Things were looking up. Settling herself behind the wheel so she'd look older, she wondered which boy Sharon would leave for her.

Sharon struck up a conversation, deftly evading the boys' questions, a tactic that made her seem mysterious. When the blond guy asked where she lived, Sharon replied, "Around," and when the other boy asked what school she went to Sharon simply laughed.

Nobody paid any attention to Jackie. Apparently she hadn't fooled anyone by sitting in the driver's seat. Disappointed, she fiddled with the keychain dangling from the ignition and then she poked her finger in the different-sized holes in the chrome spokes radiating out from the hub of the steering wheel. Would her pinky finger fit in the smallest hole? She thrust it in and then, to her horror, discovered she could not get it *out*.

She tugged and pulled but her finger wouldn't come free. "Sharon — "

"Shhhh." Her sister made an impatient don't-bother-me gesture.

"Sharon, my finger is stuck in the steering wheel."

"Well, pull it out," Sharon said, not even looking at her. She was giving the blond guy that smile that showed her dimples.

"I can't. It's *stuck*." She yanked again, but her finger was firmly wedged in the hole. Panic welled up in her. Suppose she never got her finger out of the steering wheel? How would she be able to go to school? She imagined herself lugging the steering wheel around the rest of her life.

"Help me!" she shrieked.

Sharon whirled around. "What *is* it? For Pete's sakes, what have you done now?"

"I can't get my finger out!" Jackie wailed.

Her sister stared at Jackie's finger caught in the steering wheel. "Why on earth did you stick your finger in that hole, anyway? Honestly, Jackie."

"Hurry! My finger is swelling!"

Sharon slid across the seat. "All right . . . I'm going to push your hand in, then give a big yank, so be ready."

She pushed Jackie's hand. The horn blared. Jackie started to cry. Her finger was killing her and now the horn wouldn't stop. The boys in the next car laughed hysterically.

The carhop brought their food. She hooked the tray over the door and left, shaking her head.

"What am I going to do?" Jackie bawled. "My finger hurts!"

"Please be quiet!" Sharon said. "We need soap or something." She glanced at the foil-wrapped burgers. "Mayonnaise! We got everything on our hamburgers." Reaching across Jackie, she grabbed a hamburger, unwrapped it, then smeared a gob of mayonnaise on Jackie's hand.

It worked! Jackie pulled her hand free. Under the coating of mayonnaise, her little finger was red and swelling. "Thanks," she said, relieved. Now she wouldn't have to carry a steering wheel around for the rest of her life.

The boys in the next parking slot had gone. Sharon fumed at the lost opportunity. "They couldn't have been worth much, to let a measly thing like a stuck finger scare them off," she reasoned. "How's your hand? Does it still hurt?"

Jackie gingerly wiped her throbbing finger on a napkin. "A little."

"What did you do such a dumb thing for?"

To say she'd just been fooling around would make her sound even dumber, so Jackie replied, "I just wanted to do something impulsive."

"Well, that was certainly impulsive." Sharon made a face as she cleaned the mayonnaise-slicked steering wheel. Then she began laughing. "I can't take you *anywhere*!"

"Is that why I never go anywhere?" Jackie laughed, too. It *was* funny, now that her finger didn't hurt so much. A sore finger was a small sacrifice, she thought, if it helped bring her and Sharon together again.

Chapter 8

The weeks between Thanksgiving and Christmas flew by and soon it was the date Jackie's mother had circled in red on the calendar.

"Sharon comes home today," Mrs. Howard said joyfully at breakfast. "She'll be here when you get home from school. Jackie! You haven't bought your sister a Christmas present yet," she said with a degree of alarm that Jackie equated with something really important.

"I don't know what to get her," Jackie replied glumly. She had already bought a set of daisy potholders and matching toaster cover for her mother and a pipe stand for her father. "Sharon's so picky."

While Jackie was the type to become ecstatic over a fresh bag of Cheetos, Sharon turned her nose up at anything less than "good stuff." Good stuff to Sharon meant presents like electric razors, phony fur jackets, black strapless dresses, and cars, all out of Jackie's price range.

Jackie remembered one Christmas Eve when their parents were out. Sharon expertly slipped the wrapping off the few remaining presents she hadn't already sneaked open. One was a pair of gloves from Aunt Helen, a perfectly nice pair of winter gloves for a young girl, warm and practical. But because they weren't studded with rhinestones, Sharon sniffed disdainfully, then crammed the gloves back in the box.

Jackie felt bad for poor Aunt Helen, who had probably searched far and wide for those gloves. "No, she didn't," Sharon said. "She picked them up on sale somewhere. Probably bought a dozen pairs to give to all her nieces. I bet you got a pair, too." Jackie glanced at the glove-sized box with her name on it and vowed to squeal with rapture when she opened hers Christmas morning, to make up for Sharon's rudeness.

During lunch at school that day, Jackie discussed her problem with her friends. "I have no idea what to get my sister," she said woefully. "And time is running out. Christmas is Tuesday."

"I have the same problem," Frieda said, "only multiplied by three. No, two. My little brother is easy to buy for. He likes anything that makes a lot of noise."

"Get her a book," suggested Carol. "That's what I'm buying the people on my list this year."

Carol loved to read and fervently believed everyone else should, too.

"Well, we know what we're getting from Carol," Paula quipped.

"Make mine steamy," Jackie said. Then she remarked, "Sharon wouldn't like a book, even a steamy one, unless it was about her."

"You're making too much of this," said Frieda. "Just buy her some cologne and let it go at that."

"It's my mother's fault," Jackie said. "She goes into a tailspin every time Sharon comes home from school. Is it like that at your house when Wayne comes home from Madison?"

"Are you kidding? My mom's been baking a solid week, all the things Wayne likes, which means everybody has to eat Wayne's favorites. But Wayne doesn't act big-headed or anything. It's just my mother who makes such a fuss."

Jackie nodded. "My mother makes a fuss, but Sharon acts like she expects it. You'd think she was visiting royalty." She sighed, no closer to a solution. "I'll have to go shopping tomorrow. The stores will be jammed. No, Sharon will ask me right away if I've got her present yet and when she finds out I haven't, she'll march me to the stores. You wait."

But when Jackie got home that afternoon, Sharon was asleep on the sofa, a box of Kleenex on her chest. The coffee table was cluttered with cough syrup, more tissues, throat lozenges, sticky spoons, glasses of ginger ale, and magazines.

Mrs. Howard tiptoed in from the kitchen. "She

has a terrible cold. Living in that drafty old apartment. I wouldn't be surprised if it doesn't go into pneumonia."

Jackie rolled her eyes heavenward. If she'd been sick, she would have a common, garden-variety cold, but Sharon was clearly ready for intensive care. Her mother went back into the kitchen, probably to whip up something for the patient.

A coughing fit woke Sharon. "Hey, Bony Maronie," she croaked, blowing her nose vigorously. "What'd you buy me for Christmas?"

"I knew it!" Jackie cried. "I knew you'd ask me that!"

"Well, what'd you buy me?" Even on her deathbed, Sharon wasn't about to be cheated out of a present.

"I'm not telling. What did you buy me?" Jackie countered.

"I'm not telling."

They stared at each other. Then Jackie remarked, "You cut your hair. And it isn't black anymore."

"I dyed it back natural," Sharon said, which sounded like a contradiction to Jackie. How could anything be natural if it was dyed? With her short, dark hair feathered against her pale cheeks, Sharon looked older, more worldly. Lying back in a nest of pillows, her brown eyes glittered with fever and the germ of an idea. "Short hair is much easier to manage. You ought to let me cut yours," she said enticingly.

"Oh, no! It's taken me a whole year to grow

my hair. I'm not about to cut it now." Jackie swished her long ponytail. "You're not experimenting on me."

Another spasm of coughs racked Sharon's body. "You ought to be ashamed," Sharon said. "This might be the last haircut I ever give."

"How do you feel?"

"Terrible." Tired of blowing, Sharon stuffed a tissue in each nostril and left them there. "You know what would make me feel better?"

"What?" Jackie guessed her sister wanted a cookie or more ice for her ginger ale.

"Tell me what Mom and Dad got me for Christmas."

"Sharon! Christmas is Tuesday. Can't you wait four more days?"

"I might not live that long. I want to know *now*." Jackie couldn't believe her sister would be eighteen in a few weeks. "Don't you feel sorry for your poor sick sister?" She coughed again for emphasis. "Just give me a little hint. Will I like it?"

Jackie clamped her lips shut.

"I'd tell you if you asked me," Sharon said, switching to a belligerent tone. Then she went back to what she did best, wheedling. "Just tell me one teeny hint. Pretty please with sugar on top? Listen, if you tell me what Mom got me, I'll tell you what I got you."

"I don't want to know. I want to be surprised on Christmas Day," Jackie said flatly. "Every year you spoil Christmas with your snooping and making me tell you what Mama got you until I practically have to gag myself."

Sharon wasn't about to give up. "Okay, tell me what you got me."

"I haven't gotten you anything yet."

Sharon leaped off the pillows. "You haven't bought my present yet! What kind of sister are you, waiting till the last minute!"

"I don't know what to buy you. You're so hard to buy for. What do you want?" Jackie asked.

Her sister reclined again, pleased to be classified difficult-to-buy-for. "Well, there are a few things I'd like."

"What are they?" Jackie half expected her sister to whip out a list typed in triplicate. "Remember, I don't have much money."

"I guess not, at this late date. Maybe you can borrow more from Mom." Sharon casually examined a thumbnail. "I'd like a new bedroom suite — "

"Furniture! Sharon, do you think I'm a millionaire?"

" — I'm sick of sleeping on that saggy old daybed in the apartment," Sharon went on, blithely ignoring Jackie's protests. "If you don't get me that, I'd like some French lingerie. Or some really good perfume, name-brand, not the kind you buy in the drug store."

Bedroom furniture and French lingerie! Only an insufferable creep would demand such outrageous gifts. Jackie went into the kitchen and circled another date on the calendar with the red marker, the day Sharon was scheduled to leave again.

Saturday, Mrs. Howard took Sharon to the doctor, who diagnosed her cold as bronchitis. As bad as that sounded, Mrs. Howard wasn't satisfied until she bullied the doctor into admitting that bronchitis *could* develop into pneumonia, but the antibiotics and bed rest he prescribed for Sharon would prevent the worst from happening.

There was no time for a Christmas shopping expedition. Jackie had to buy Sharon's present at the drug store while Sharon's prescriptions were being filled. She took Frieda's advice and got Sharon cologne, the best the store carried. The cologne came boxed with a travel-size version in a cute teddy-bear bottle, which Jackie thought made up for it being purchased in a drug store. With her last dollar, she added a huge candy cane to the package.

Sharon refused to stay in the guest room, claiming it was too depressing away from everyone. Mrs. Howard made up a bed in the living room, where Sharon wouldn't miss the holiday activities and could be coddled even more. She coughed like a seal, mostly at night so she could keep everybody awake. Jackie thought about Beth in *Little Women*, who was dying of tuberculosis but remained noble to the end. In contrast, Sharon was a perfectly repulsive invalid.

On Sunday, Sharon felt well enough to help

Jackie decorate the Christmas tree Mr. Howard set up in front of the picture window. Mrs. Howard announced she and Mr. Howard were going to deliver presents to the Perkinses.

"Sharon, be sure to take your pill at four. And don't stay up too long, you're still weak," Mrs. Howard said. "We'll be over there an hour or so, but if you need anything, give me a call."

Sharon coughed feebly.

"When you come back, Mama, we'll have the tree finished," Jackie said happily, trying to spread a little holiday cheer. All this sickroom talk was making her own throat feel scratchy.

"It looks nice already," her mother said, barely flicking a glance in her direction. "Now, Sharon, take it easy. Let Jackie do all the reaching."

Sure, let Jackie, who was six inches shorter than Sharon, stand on the wobbly stool and wind a string of tangled electric lights around the top of the tree that grazed the ceiling.

Their parents were hardly out the door when Sharon snapped to attention like one of those automatic umbrellas and said, in a voice that held no trace of feebleness, "Jackie, don't put all the blue lights on the same side."

"Am I doing that?" Jackie stepped back to view her work. The lights *were* all on one side. She shifted the strand.

Sharon sorted through the boxes of decorations. "Where are the bubble lights?"

"In the brown box." Jackie hummed "We Three Kings," feeling warm and Christmasy. At last they were actually doing something to-gether. She imagined they looked like a Norman Rockwell painting.

"I don't see them," Sharon said.

"You're not looking. They're in the box right by your foot." Jackie's warm Christmas feeling cooled a bit.

"No, they aren't. Oh, there they are." Sharon lifted out the antique lights. "They ought to go in the front where we can see them."

"We usually hang them close to the top," Jackie reminded her. They had decorated the tree for umpteen years. Didn't Sharon remember?

"Not this year. I want to put them where *I* want," Sharon said stubbornly.

"What *you* want? What about what *I* want? Or Mama and Daddy? Who died and left you king?" Jackie was angry. They always did things a cer-tain way. Why did Sharon want to change the ritual? Suddenly Jackie dropped the strand of blue lights and snatched the box from Sharon.

Sharon grabbed the box back. "I'm putting these lights in the front, Jackie, whether you like it or not."

Jackie leaped for the box but Sharon held it over her head. Giving up, Jackie said sourly, "All right, *put* the dumb old lights on the tree, see what I care. Anyway, Mama said I could have them when I got older."

Sharon propped the candle-shaped bulbs on the branches where they would be most noticed. When the lights were plugged in, the heat caused fluid to bubble up into the colored glass cylinders. "Nuh-uh. I asked for the bubble lights a long time ago. Mom said I could have them."

This threw Jackie into a rage. Holiday spirit, in short supply anyway, and togetherness were forgotten as she shrieked, "You can't have the lights! They're *mine*! You got the Melmac dishes and everything else around here, but those lights are MINE."

Sharon stared at her. "What in the world is wrong with you? You're grumpier than I am and I'm the one who's sick."

Jackie didn't answer, but dug through the assorted boxes. Since Sharon had wrecked the bubble-light ritual, she was determined to hang the stockings from the fireplace mantle. She found hers, a long red flannel sock with "Jackie" written in glitter on the turned-down part. "Where's your dumb old stocking?" Jackie asked Sharon. "I can't find it."

"It's at the apartment," Sharon replied, repositioning a bubble light that kept flopping over.

Jackie rocked back on her heels. Sharon's stocking was in Harrisonburg? "The apartment? What's it doing there?"

"I wrote Mom and asked her to send it. The other girls were doing a little decorating and I wanted something from home. I was going to bring it back with me but I left it there."

"Why'd you do that?" Jackie said, upset. "Now we only have one stocking to hang from the mantle. It looks stupid." No "Sharon" stocking to go with the "Jackie" stocking. It was going to be a terrible Christmas. She began to cry, silent tears spilling down her cheeks.

"Good grief, Jackie, it's nothing to cry over. I'll go get one of Dad's socks. That's almost as good."

"No, it isn't!"

"Jackie, what is *wrong* with you? It's only a stocking."

It wasn't the stocking, or the bubble lights, or her sister's bronchitis. Jackie attempted to sort her jumbled feelings. She wanted them to get along, like two sisters in a Christmas card. After all, it was the season to be merry. But Sharon took over like a storm trooper, making demands, and worse, ignoring their old traditions. Her sister had ruined Jackie's Christmas.

Her sobs slowed to sniffles. "It's — it's the pressure of the holidays," she said, using the excuse her mother relied on when she was snippish from baking cookies, wrapping presents, and addressing cards all at once.

Sharon sat down beside her. "Look, I put the bubble lights on wrong," she said, making amends. "Why don't you straighten them out? You're better at that than I am."

"They look fine to me."

"I know! Let's get into the presents," Sharon said suddenly, as if she'd just thought of it, but Jackie knew that finding out what she was getting for Christmas had been uppermost in her sister's mind for days. "I'll open one and you open one."

"No," Jackie said firmly. "You made me do

that once and I was miserable, because I wasn't surprised on Christmas morning."

"I didn't *make* you, either. I opened one and then you begged me to open one of yours because you'd rip the paper."

"And I *hated* what I'd done the minute I did it!" Tears came to her eyes again. "It's not the same anymore, Sharon. Nothing's the same anymore, and I don't know why."

Sharon put her arm around Jackie. "I know. It's hard for me, too. The girls put up a tree at the apartment and it made me so homesick. That's why I asked Mom to send me my stocking. But it didn't look right, either, hanging from a nail on the wall instead of our mantle."

"I don't think I like Christmas anymore." Jackie leaned into her sister's shoulder.

"You're just saying that because you're blue. Everybody's a little sad around the holidays."

"Not little kids," Jackie said.

"Which means you're not a little kid anymore. Just look at that tree," Sharon said. "Is this the prettiest tree we've ever had, or what?"

Jackie let out a deep breath that seemed to have been pent up for days. It *was* a pretty tree. And the bubble lights did look better where Sharon had put them. Maybe it was time to do things a bit differently. She sat peacefully with her sister, fascinated by the bubbling lights the way she'd been when she was little.

After a while, she felt better.

Chapter 9

"I despise the week between Christmas and New Year's," Sharon said the day after Christmas. "It's so boring."

Recovered from her illness, Sharon picked at the tree, at her hair, at the fruitcake on the kitchen table in a restless, aimless manner. She had just finished hanging the nonbreakable ornaments along the bottom branches so her cat could bat them. Now she removed the tinsel that Jackie had so carefully draped among the branches, tossing it back on the tree willy-nilly.

Jackie liked the final week of the year. She looked upon the odd, leftover days after Christmas as an opportunity to think about what she had done the past year and what she'd like to do in the coming year. So far this year she hadn't accomplished much toward her goal of becoming her own person. She was thinking about starting over with a new identity, since the old one wasn't working.

"At least you're invited out on New Year's Eve," Jackie said, nesting her emptied gift boxes. She had already folded the tissue paper for her mother to save and re-use. "I have to sit home again."

"If you had some real friends, you'd probably have an invitation," Sharon remarked.

"My friends *are* real," Jackie argued. "Just because they don't carry on half the night like yours do doesn't mean they aren't nice." She stacked her presents in a tower, preparing to take them to her room.

Sharon stopped throwing tinsel. "What are you doing?"

"Putting my presents away. Christmas is over."

"For one day. Honestly, Jackie, you are so compulsive. Putting your Christmas presents away barely the day after Christmas." Her sister shook her head, as if Jackie were a hopeless case.

Actually, Jackie would have put her things in her room as soon as she opened them. Once the wrappings were off the presents, the tree no longer looked festive, especially after Sharon started messing with it. Brightly wrapped gifts heaped around the tree were mysterious and exciting; plain white boxes sitting in groups — Jackie's pile, Sharon's pile, her parents' pile — seemed pitiful and not the least bit Christmasy. Even the bare tree would look better than those stark white boxes sitting around it. But her mother objected. "Leave our things out so people who come to see us can look at them." That was something else Jackie didn't like, having other people, even her own relatives, paw through her Christmas presents. She wasn't stingy, just private.

She took exception to Sharon's comment. "If I'm compulsive, then you're a slob. You'd leave your stuff on the floor till the next Christmas. At least Mama doesn't have to yell at me."

"Still the goody-goody, aren't you?" Sharon said mildly. She sat down to review her gifts for about the forty-third time. Even though she did not receive a new bedroom suite or French lingerie, Sharon adored her presents. The quilted satin coverlet and the miniature refrigerator were "absolutely perfect." Her drab apartment would be transformed into a penthouse, she'd exaggerated, kissing her parents. And she squealed with delight over Jackie's cologne, spraying it on herself, on Jackie, on their mother, even on the cat. Sharon was *so* hard to figure out, Jackie thought.

She glanced down at her own little pile. Her gifts were more numerous than Sharon's but not as grand. This had caused a minor outcry on Christmas Eve, when the girls sorted the presents and counted them. "You've got twelve and I've only got five!" Sharon exclaimed. Sharon's ruffled feathers were smoothed on Christmas morning when Mr. Howard brought in the enormous box that contained the miniature refrigerator.

Jackie loved her parents' gifts, a red leather-bound diary, a new skirt and sweater, and a jewelry box, but Sharon's present, a bracelet with dangling pink stones and a little gold heart inscribed "October," puzzled her. It was obviously a birthstone bracelet, but Jackie's birthday was in *September*.

"Do you like it?" Sharon had asked eagerly. "The minute I saw it I thought of you."

Jackie tried to keep her face neutral. She always had a tough time with presents that didn't quite suit her, unlike her sister who quickly pointed out if something was the wrong size or an unflattering color. Should she tell Sharon she'd bought the wrong month? Didn't her sister *know* Jackie's birthday was in September? She certainly ought to. How many sister's birthdays did she have to remember? On the other hand, Jackie didn't want to appear displeased and hurt Sharon's feelings.

"It's — it's very pretty," she'd stammered, holding the bracelet up to the light. Maybe Sharon never *noticed* there was writing on the gold heart. Maybe if she pretended she'd just noticed it herself, she'd save her sister from embarrassment. "Oh, look!" she said casually. "There's writing on the heart. It says . . . 'October.' "

Mrs. Howard came over to examine the bracelet. "It does say October. It's a birthstone bracelet. Sharon, did you know you got an October bracelet for Jackie?"

"They were out of September," Sharon said slightly embarrassed. "I like the stones for October better. Don't you, Jackie?"

Jackie didn't know what to think. It wasn't a mistake — Sharon had deliberately bought her a birthstone bracelet for the wrong month. She couldn't exchange it. Sharon had purchased it at some store in Harrisonburg, and anyway, Sharon seemed certain she had bought just the right present for Jackie.

Now she put the bracelet in one of the trays in her new jewelry box. She planned to rearrange the items on her vanity table, using the jewelry box as a centerpiece.

Sharon watched her. "Aren't you going to wear the bracelet I got you?"

"Well — I was going to clean my room."

"When are you going to wear it?" Sharon pressed.

"When I go someplace special," Jackie replied. "I'd wear it New Year's Eve if I was going out but I'm not."

"Wear it anyway. Wear it today. Somebody might come over this afternoon." Sharon took the bracelet from the jewelry box and clasped it around Jackie's wrist. The pink stones glittered in the December sunlight filtering through the picture window. "There. You look positively elegant. It *is* pretty, isn't it?"

Jackie stared at the bracelet. She felt strange wearing someone else's birthstones, as if *she* had made a mistake and been born in the wrong month. "I'm going to clean my room now," she said to Sharon. "What are you going to do?"

"I don't know," Sharon sighed. "I hate this week. I wish I was back at school."

"I thought you liked being home." Who wouldn't like being waited on hand and foot, having her every whim catered to by doting parents?

Sharon followed Jackie into her room and sat on the bed. "I did at first because I was sick. But I have so much to do, it's a waste of time to be here. No offense."

"None taken." Jackie set the new jewelry box in the middle of her vanity table. Then she began arranging her cat figurines around the jewelry box. "If you have so much to do, why don't you do some of your studying here?"

"Too many distractions." Sharon lounged against Jackie's pillow. "Mom popping in every two seconds to ask if I want a cookie or some eggnog. The phone ringing."

Such a bore, having all those friends call. "I thought it was like that at your apartment in Harrisonburg, people running in and out all the time." Jackie placed her best figurine, a white china cat that once graced the top of Sharon's ninth birthday cake, in front of the mirror.

"That's different. I don't know what it is about being home, but I don't feel like working. Besides, I really need to be getting my hours in at the beauty academy and it's closed this week." Sharon got up and circled her old room, touching objects as if reacquainting herself with her own past. She sighed again. "I guess I'll go study a little."

Jackie hung up her new skirt, thinking about her sister. Sharon drifted around the house like a ship without a rudder. At night Jackie could hear measured *whump-whump* sounds from next door, and knew Sharon was having trouble getting to sleep. Whenever her sister couldn't sleep, she would lie on her stomach and raise one foot off the mattress, then let it fall, *whump*, over and over, until she was worn out.

The only present that remained to be put away was the red-leather diary. Jackie sat down at the vanity to fill in the "All About Me" page of the diary. She wrote her name, address, the names of her parents and her sister, but paused over the line that inquired about a pet. Felix really belonged to Sharon but he still lived at home, like Jackie. More and more the cat came to Jackie's room to have her scratch the itchy spot under his chin and snooze on her bed. Finally she wrote, "Felix, my part-time cat."

The shallow vanity drawer was the ideal place to store her diary. Sharon had kept hers there. When Jackie slid the drawer open, she saw something was already in it, a folded piece of paper and a fragment of an eggshell. The Sister Pact! She had forgotten all about it. And the ancient Easter egg Sharon broke before she left for college.

Jackie unfolded the paper. *We, the undersigned, do hereby declare we will be friends through thick and*

*thin, in sickness or in health, for richer or poorer, until
death do us part.* Their signatures made it official.
As she put the document back in the drawer,
her bracelet tinkled with the movement, the pink
October stones catching the light.

She hadn't acted very friendly since Sharon
came home. They lived in the same house, but
they kept missing each other, almost like the
time Sharon and her friend Linda decided to hike
through the woods behind the Howard house
to a store on Route 50. They told Mrs. Howard
they were just going as far as the creek to see if
it had frozen over, but when they were gone
two hours, Mrs. Howard slipped into her coat
to hunt for them. Left behind, Jackie paced from
window to door as shadows lengthened over the
snow-covered yard. Suppose her mother never
came back? Suppose none of them ever came
back? Jackie grabbed her own coat and ran outside into the wintry twilight. She stumbled
through the snowy woods, but no one answered
her call. At last she returned home, astonished
to find Sharon and Linda and her mother already
there, laughing at the mix-up. They had all been
in the woods at the same time, looking for each
other, but their paths never crossed.

Maybe, Jackie decided, they should add a
clause to the Sister Pact, that they'd be friends
through thick and thin, in sickness and in health,
even during the Christmas holidays.

She went into the guest room. Sharon was
lying on the bed with her blue beauty school
textbook. She looked up at Jackie.

"If it'll help, you can practice hairstyles on me," Jackie suggested. "Or facials or whatever. You said you need to practice."

Flipping the book aside, Sharon jumped to her feet. "Great! Go wet your hair and meet me in the kitchen."

Soon Jackie was seated on two phone books on a kitchen chair, swathed in a towel. Sharon raked the tangles out of her hair, none too gently, and discussed what she would do to Jackie.

"I'm going to try fingerwaves at the crown and stand-up curls on top," she said, sectioning Jackie's hair with the end of a rat-tail comb.

"Fingerwaves," Mrs. Howard commented with astonishment. "Why, those haven't been in style for years and years."

"I know. But my instructor told us that's what we have to do to pass Virginia state boards. It's to show dexterity or something. Some old lady might come in and want fingerwaves, you never can tell." She pushed Jackie's hair into waves, then set it with clips. "You know, Jackie, you've got pretty good hair."

"What do you mean?"

"It takes fingerwaves. Not everybody's hair does that." Sharon undid a clip, then ran her fingers through the curl. "See, Mom, how her hair holds a curl? She'd be a good model to take to my board exam this spring."

"What's this about a model?" Mrs. Howard asked.

"I have to take a model with me," Sharon explained. "Someone to work on. It's not just a written test — I have to do hairstyles and some other stuff on a real live person. Each student must provide her own model. It's the rule. If I don't have a model, I can't take the exam. And I can't drag somebody in off the street. It's either you or Jackie. I'd take you but your hair's too short. And too gray. Gray hair is hard to work with."

"It's no fun to have, either." Mrs. Howard glanced at Jackie, then Sharon. "Where is the exam?"

"Richmond." Sharon spoke with the comb between her teeth.

"Oh, boy!" Jackie cried. "I get to go to Richmond!"

Mrs. Howard was less than elated with the proposition. "Why don't you take one of the girls you're rooming with?"

"Two of the girls are studying at the academy with me, so they'll probably go when I do, if we all get our hours in. And Brenda has terrible hair, fine and limp, like baby hair. I can't do a thing with it. Jackie is perfect."

Jackie glowed with her sister's praise. She knew Sharon meant her *hair*, but it still sounded nice to hear she was perfect.

"I don't know," Mrs. Howard said. "Going all the way to Richmond . . ."

"I have to take *some*body. And I want to pass my boards, so I should take somebody with good

107

hair. Richmond isn't that far. We'll only be gone a day."

Mrs. Howard gave in by degrees, the way she always did. "Well, I suppose your father could drive us down one Saturday and we could browse in antique shops while you and Jackie — "

Sharon interrupted. "Mom, my state board exam *can't* be a family excursion. First of all, the boards are held on a weekday, and second, I don't want the whole family trooping down there. I'll be nervous enough — "

"Held during the week?" Mrs. Howard repeated. "Jackie can't go."

"Why not?" Jackie piped up.

"Why not?" echoed Sharon.

"Because she'll miss a school day. You can't miss school, Jackie," her mother told her.

"One day!" Sharon protested. "Good grief, Mom, it's not like Jackie is flunking or anything. She can miss one day and the world won't come to an end. Besides, going to Richmond will be very educational."

"I want to go!" Jackie yelled.

"There's no need to shout." To Sharon Mrs. Howard said, "All right. But we're going to set some ground rules about this trip. If you want to take Jackie, you'll have to obey us. Is that clear?"

"Sure," Sharon promised quickly. She rapped the back of Jackie's head with the comb. "Hey, Bony Maronie. You're my model."

Jackie bounced off the phone books. "I'm

going to Richmond to be a model!" She was taking a real trip! Okay, so Richmond wasn't New York City, but it was outside Fairfax County. She was finally going someplace!

She danced around her sister, making her October bracelet jingle. "Look!" she cried happily. "Isn't my new bracelet pretty?"

"I knew you'd like it," Sharon said. "The minute I saw it."

Chapter 10

"What is that you have on your head?" Mrs. Howard asked Jackie at breakfast.

"Your old Easter hat." Jackie adjusted the brim so she could see her plate.

"You're not wearing that to school?" her mother said in a tone that implied Jackie would be committing fashion suicide if she did.

The ends of the navy grosgrain ribbon that encircled the hat brim fell over Jackie's eyes. She pushed them back to look pleadingly at her mother. "I can, can't I? I won't get it dirty or anything."

Her mother poured herself more coffee. "You never told me you were in a play today."

"I'm not. I just — need to wear this hat." Her mother's old Easter hat was an important part of Jackie's revised plan. Today was the first day of school after the Christmas holidays. Everybody would be wearing new clothes, talking about what they had done over the holidays. Now was the time for Jackie to reveal the new, improved Jackie Howard.

"Yes, you may have my hat," her mother said. "It looks kind of silly, though, to wear a spring hat in January. And the style is years too old for you."

Jackie didn't care. The hat was only a prop. Once her friends learned why she was wearing a hat in the first place, it wouldn't matter if it were a ten-gallon Stetson.

At school, she found Frieda waiting by her locker. "Your bus was late — " Frieda began. "Hey, why the hat? Are you trying to start a new fad? Make sure Celeste Wellington sees you. Maybe she'll go home and get her mother's hat, too."

"I'm wearing this hat for a reason," Jackie said evenly, spinning the combination on her locker. She had to hold her head up in order to keep the hat from sliding down over her eyes, which meant she couldn't see the numbers on the dial. Not wanting to appear stupid in front of Frieda, Jackie decided to fake it. "Darn, this locker is jammed again. I guess I'll have to go to the office and report it."

"Here, let me try. What's your combination?"

Jackie whispered the three-digit code to Frieda, who whirled the dial to the correct positions and opened Jackie's locker with ease.

"It wasn't jammed at all," she said. "You must

have dialed the wrong combination. That happens to me sometimes. Why are you wearing that hat?"

"It's a long story," Jackie replied, pulling out the books she'd need for her morning classes. "I'll tell you at lunch. Then I can tell everybody."

"You don't have a bald spot, do you?" Frieda guessed. "Listen, it's nothing to be ashamed of. My cousin had scarlet fever really bad and her hair fell out. Only a little of it grew back in — "

"I'm not bald," Jackie reassured her. "In fact, it's just the opposite. See you and the others at lunch. Save me a seat."

Just as she knew it would, her hat attracted stares as she entered the classroom. Some laughed and made cracks but Jackie sailed to her desk, giving the wisecrackers a fishy stare that silenced them.

In French, Adair McConnell remarked that the Easter parade was early this year. Jackie was afraid the teacher might make fun of her, but then he added that her flowery *chapeau* on a gray winter's day was like a breath of spring. Jackie blushed at his compliment and figured the other girls, who could barely keep from swooning whenever Adair McConnell glanced in their direction, were sure to raid their mothers' closets before nightfall.

True to her word, Frieda saved Jackie a seat in the cafeteria. Paula and Carol, undoubtedly primed by Frieda, goggled at Jackie as she sat down with her tray.

"Okay," Frieda said. "I've waited long

enough. Practically everybody in school is talking about your hat. *Why* are you wearing it?"

Jackie had rehearsed her speech in her mind at least ten times. "Well," she began, pleased to have their undivided attention. "You know how hand models have to wear gloves all the time to protect their hands — "

"What?" Carol broke in. "Hand models? What are they?"

"Don't you guys know anything?" Jackie said. "A hand model is somebody who only uses her hands in advertisements, like the lady's hands in a dishwashing liquid commercial — "

"How come not the rest of her body?" Paula asked.

Jackie frowned. The discussion was getting off track. She had to get them back on it in a hurry or her whole point would be lost. "Maybe they've got an ugly face or fat knees. The important thing is their hands. Their hands are perfect and so valuable, they don't wash dishes or scrape paint and they wear gloves all the time so they won't break a nail."

Frieda ate a grape, then spit out the seed. "What does this have to do with your hat?"

"If you'll let me *finish*, I'll *tell* you," Jackie replied testily. With all the interruptions, she forgot how she was going to get from hand models and their gloves to the reason she was wearing her mother's old Easter hat. "Well, it's the same with hair models," she said, plunging ahead. "Their hair is a valuable asset and they have to protect it so nothing will happen to it."

113

She stopped to let this fact sink in.

Carol lightly tapped the brim of Jackie's hat. "You mean you're wearing this hat to protect your hair? Why?"

"Because," Jackie finished loudly. "I'm a hair model!"

Frieda dropped her grapes in disbelief. "You are not!"

"I am, too! I'm going to Richmond in a couple of months to be a hair model for my sister's board exam. I have perfect hair, she said, and I'm the only one she can take." Jackie doffed the hat with impeccable timing and shook her long, lustrous hair, the valuable hair that would ensure her sister a hairdresser's certificate.

"It looks like regular hair to me," Frieda remarked, frowning. "I don't see what's so special about your hair."

Of course she wouldn't, with her Brillo-pad hair. "It's the texture," Jackie explained, pulling a lock forward between two fingers. "Sharon did some styles on me, and my hair holds finger-waves and pincurls. Hardly anybody's does."

"Fingerwaves!" Carol sputtered. "What is that? Who gets their hair fingerwaved?"

"Probably nobody, but Sharon still has to know how to do it or she won't pass her boards. The last thing Sharon told me was to take good care of my hair. Her future as hairdresser to the stars depends on it." Actually, the last thing Sharon told Jackie before she left for Harrisonburg was to go wash her face, she had a streak of dirt on her nose, but Sharon *would* have told her to take

114

care of her hair if she had thought of it.

"I've never met a hair model before," Paula said, impressed.

"You still haven't," Frieda scoffed. "Jackie isn't a model — her sister is just going to do fingerwaves and stuff on her hair to pass a test. Nobody else will see her." To Jackie she said scornfully, "You make it sound like you're going to be on TV, selling shampoo or something."

"I might," Jackie said loftily. "You don't know everything, Frieda Jamison. I will too be seen, by the judges. Who do you think they get to judge these things? Professional hair people, that's who. Famous hairdressers and people who make hair products. Mr. Revlon himself could be one of the judges." Frieda had unwittingly added a new facet to Jackie's story. Impulsively, she expanded on her original idea.

"This is what will happen," she speculated. "Sharon will be working on my hair, making the most fantastic fingerwaves anyone ever made. The judges will rush over, give her the highest marks, and then they'll realize the model has perfect hair, just right for television! And I'll be discovered!"

"Oh, my gosh," Paula breathed. "When are you going to Richmond?"

"In the spring, after Sharon has enough hours."

"Can you get us on TV?" Carol asked.

Jackie smiled. "Sure. I won't forget you guys when I'm a famous model. After all, you knew me when."

"When you were just ordinary Jackie Howard," Frieda muttered. "Anyway, I bet Mr. Revlon is dead." She wadded her lunch bag and got up abruptly to throw it in the trash.

"Frieda's mad," Carol observed. "I wonder what's eating her?"

"Some people can't handle another person's success," Jackie said.

In no time, Jackie became a minor freshman celebrity. The story raged around the school like a forest fire, blown out of proportion. People gossiped about how a talent scout spotted Jackie walking around the shopping center and auditioned her for a shampoo commercial. Jackie changed her Easter hat to her father's navy watch cap and then a felt beret to keep interest at a fever pitch. In the girls' room between classes, she brushed her hair very carefully, often drawing a knot of admirers who made room for her in front of the mirrors. Her hair became legendary, described as an unusual shade of chestnut and measured in the locker room during PE to see how much it had grown from one day to the next. Girls in shampoo commercials always had hair that tumbled halfway to their waists so they could fling it around and show how clean it was.

Carol and Paula appointed themselves as Jackie's chief hair protectors, shielding her hair with their books during a fire drill, in case a shower of sparks suddenly rained down, and pinning

Jackie's hair on top of her head before PE, so it wouldn't get snarled in volleyball.

"Lady Godiva's hair didn't get this much attention," Frieda complained one day in late February. "You guys acted like idiots, holding your books over Jackie's head that time in the parking lot. The school wasn't even on fire!"

"It could have been," Paula said defensively. "Jackie can't afford to have her hair singed."

"When are you going to Richmond anyway?" Frieda asked Jackie.

"Probably the end of March. Sharon might be ready to go during spring break," Jackie answered, although Sharon's sketchy letters home indicated the opposite. Her sister was inundated with work at the university while scrambling to acquire her hours at the beauty academy.

"Well, I'll be glad when you go," Frieda said, "because when you come back, you'll be a normal person again."

"What's that supposed to mean?" Jackie demanded.

"You figure it out. That is, if your brain hasn't collapsed under all that valuable hair." Turning, Frieda walked away from them.

"Don't let her upset you," Carol said. "She's just jealous."

Jackie said nothing. Frieda had been impossible lately, hardly ever calling Jackie after school like she used to. From the beginning, Frieda controlled their little group, and now that Paula and Carol were siding with Jackie, Frieda

117

snubbed them all. There was only room at the top for one and that was Jackie. She intended to stay there, no matter what Frieda thought.

"I bet my hair's grown at least an inch since Sharon was here," Jackie speculated that afternoon, staring at her reflection in the bathroom mirror.

Her mother was scrubbing the tub. "If you don't quit fussing with that hair, I'm going to scream. By the way, I got a letter from Sharon today."

"Really? What'd she say? Are we going to Richmond during spring break?"

Her mother swished the sponge around the tub with maddening deliberation. "She's not coming home for spring break. She needs that time at the academy to get more hours." Her mother sounded disappointed. Sharon wasn't able to come home on her eighteenth birthday, either.

"So we're not going in March," Jackie concluded.

Mrs. Howard straightened up to look at her. "You're not going at all. Sharon has decided to take her landlady to Richmond as her model."

"WHAT!"

"Don't yell at me," her mother scolded. "You can read the letter for yourself. She said her landlady has better hair and she wants to take her instead."

Sharon's landlady had better hair? No one had hair as good as Jackie's! Jackie's hair was *perfect*, her fingerwaves never drooped.

"Can I call Sharon?" she asked her mother.

"You may not. We've had too many long-distance calls lately. The phone bill will be out of sight this month."

"But this is an emergency! I have to talk to her, find out what happened. Maybe — "

"Jackie, she's already made up her mind. She's taking her landlady and that's that." Her mother's tone softened. "I know you had your heart set on going. I'm sorry."

"But everybody thinks I'm going to be Sharon's model!"

"You know what I've told you about bragging," her mother said.

Jackie knew too well. Her mother discouraged boasting in any form, to the extreme that she would listen to other parents brag about their children's accomplishments and not say a word about her own, even if they had just won the Nobel prize.

"I'm disappointed, too," Mrs. Howard said. "I wanted to see Sharon."

Well, Jackie didn't! She wasn't disappointed, she was *furious*. How could Sharon double-cross her this way? Let her believe she was the perfect hair model and then tell her somebody else was even better.

"I'm never going to do Sharon another favor as long as I live!" she proclaimed.

"Don't tell me," her mother said. "Tell Sharon. Write her a letter if you're so mad."

"I will! I'm going to write her and let her know

119

just exactly what I think of her! It'll be so long I'll have to use two stamps to mail it. Maybe more." Jackie envisioned the postman reaching into their mailbox to get the letter and falling out of his jeep from the sheer weight of it.

"At least you won't feel compelled to wear those funny hats to school now," her mother said.

Jackie remembered her new position at school. Since she wasn't going to Richmond, she wouldn't need to protect her hair anymore. She wouldn't be discovered by Mr. Revlon and flown to New York to audition for a shampoo commercial, a story she was beginning to believe herself. She'd be ordinary old Jackie Howard again. She and her hair would no longer be a celebrity. And it was all her sister's fault!

In her room, she jerked the vanity drawer open for writing paper and a pen. She considered using her nice stationery, but decided that plain old notebook paper better suited her purpose. Actually, poison ink would have suited her purpose best.

Then she saw the Sister Pact. Some forever-friend her sister turned out to be! Sharon had betrayed her. And this realization made Jackie feel even worse than losing her celebrity status at school.

With grim deliberation, Jackie ripped the document in half, and in half again. She dropped the pieces into her wastebasket, dusting her hands. She did not make pacts with creeps.

And then she burst into tears.

Chapter 11

The next week was sheer torture for Jackie. Most of the kids had stopped asking her when she was going off on her "modeling assignment," but Carol and Paula faithfully inquired, probably so they would be ready to cope with Jackie's instant stardom when she returned. Jackie guiltily evaded her friends, saying she had a lot of studying. Instead of eating lunch with them, she went to the library and miserably hunched in a chair behind the reference shelves.

Frieda found her there one day, after midterms were over and Jackie's excuse was no longer valid. "How come you don't sit with us any more?" she asked point-blank. "I guess you've gotten too good for us nonmodel types, huh?"

Her willpower to keep up the charade suddenly collapsed. "I'm not going to Richmond to be Sharon's model," Jackie said dully. "She's taking her landlady."

Frieda pretended to swoon against the Encyclopaedia Brittanicas. "Not going to Richmond! Wait'll I tell Paula — she'll be absolutely crushed. She's practically ordered business cards as your agent. And Carol, well, she'll have to give up being staff photographer on the yearbook and go back to paste-up since she won't be taking your portfolio pictures now. Maybe she can do Sharon's landlady's portfolio instead."

"Will you shut up!" Jackie cried. "It's not funny. I don't know what I'm going to do. Everybody thinks I'm going to do this great thing and now I'm not."

Frieda sat on the arm of Jackie's chair. "You have two choices," she said. "You can go on telling lies about the trip and maybe drag it out till the end of the year — that's only another couple of months. Or you can tell the truth."

There was one other choice Frieda didn't mention, the option Jackie usually took when she was in trouble. She began to cry. "If I tell the truth, everybody will laugh and then they'll hate me," she blubbered. "If I keep lying, I'll hate myself. It's all Sharon's fault! I could just kill her for doing this to me."

Frieda suddenly became sympathetic. "Gosh, Jackie, don't cry. It's really not that big a deal."

"Not to you it isn't. But my whole reputation is at stake!"

"Do you have to be a superstar to enjoy yourself? I mean, can't you just be a regular person?"

Snuffling, Jackie hunted for a tissue in her pocketbook but was unable to find one. *Did* she have to be a superstar? Where did she get such a notion in the first place? From Sharon. Sharon, the one no one ever forgot. Jackie had been competing with her sister since the day she entered high school, trying out for the drill team, finagling to get her picture in the yearbook, all things Sharon had done and was famous for. Things that did not come naturally to Jackie.

As Sharon had said after the disastrous homecoming game, not everyone shined in the limelight. Jackie recalled the time Sharon fainted in her sixth-grade class. Sharon was carried to the clinic, where she spent the rest of the day lying on the cot, plumped with pillows, reading a *Mad* magazine. Her concerned teacher checked on her every half an hour.

Jackie, who was a second-grader at the time, thought that fainting was a wonderful way to gain attention and get out of classwork. The next day she informed her teacher she was going to faint, them slumped dramatically over her desk, nearly stabbing herself with her thick, second-grader's pencil.

"If you're sick," her teacher said, "you must lie down in the nurse's office."

The nurse made her lie down on a cot on top of a paper blanket that crackled whenever Jackie moved. There were no *Mad* magazines, no one checking on her every half hour. As the afternoon wore on, Jackie wondered what her classmates were doing. Then she remembered a puppet show was coming to their class that day. She sat up to inform the nurse she was feeling better and could go back to class. The nurse pursed her mouth and replied that little girls who were sick enough to be sent to her office had to stay there until it was time to go home.

Jackie should have learned her lesson years before. What worked for Sharon tended to backfire on Jackie.

"I bet you hate me," Jackie said, sinking lower into her pit of self-pity.

"I don't hate you, even if you have been acting pretty snobby," Frieda said. "And neither will Paula or Carol. We'll help you out of this mess. We'll tell people the trip has been postponed till this summer."

"But then next fall when I come back, kids'll ask me how come I'm not a model."

"No, they won't. They'll forget all about it. Half of them won't even be at this school by then." Frieda fished a tissue from her bag and handed it to Jackie. "Wipe your face and then let's go have lunch. If Paula sees you've been crying, she'll start boo-hooing herself. You know how she is."

Laughing, Jackie mopped her tears. It felt so good to laugh with her friend again! If only she could laugh this way with her sister. But their relationship was over, finished.

As Frieda predicted, the whole affair died on its own. Basketball playoffs, the senior play, and the spring dance occupied most students' thoughts. Jackie faded back into the anonymous area with her friends, though she wished she could find a happy medium between nothingness and superstardom.

Adair McConnell, her devastatingly handsome French teacher, supplied the solution to Jackie's dilemma.

French was the one class in which Jackie consistently got A's. She loved learning a new language and sometimes daydreamed about getting a job as a translater at the United Nations or going to Paris. One Friday, as her teacher passed back test papers, he paused by Jackie's desk.

"You know, you should join the French Club," he told her. "I think you'd enjoy it, and you could help some of the others who aren't as skilled as you are."

"But it's too late," she said. "The school year is almost over."

"You could come as a guest. We're meeting this afternoon to discuss our field trip to a French restaurant. I wish you'd attend," he urged.

He was so nice, she couldn't refuse. Between fourth and fifth period, she called home and told her mother she was taking the late bus. After the last bell, she went back to Mr. McConnell's class where the French Club was held.

Outside the door, she stalled. On the list of goals she had taped to her mirror so many months before, joining a club was right after trying out for the drill team. After goofing the tryouts, she lost her nerve to join the Pep Club.

They probably wouldn't want her anyway, as Frieda was always saying. The French Club was more her level, undoubtedly packed with geeks who declined verbs for fun. Just my speed, Jackie thought as she went inside.

Adair was sitting on his desk instead of behind it, and he had taken off his jacket to establish a more informal setting. He smiled at Jackie. "Glad you could make it."

Feeling like a gate-crasher at a party, Jackie sat beside a boy she recognized from her class, Keith something-or-other. Now that she was close to him, she noticed how cute he was, the way his sandy hair swirled in an appealing cowlick.

Adair introduced her as his guest, mercifully not making her stand, and then proceeded with the meeting. The treasurer, a girl who was in Jackie's science class, reported that the April car wash was a success and they finally had enough money for the field trip.

Jackie silently counted the club members. Even with Mr. McConnell as sponsor, a huge drawing card, there were only nine members, six girls and three boys.

Mr. McConnell said, "There are many good French restaurants in D.C., but some of them are too expensive. I personally lean toward Le Provençal. It has good food at fairly reasonable prices."

For the rest of the meeting, they studied a sample French menu. Jackie shared a menu with

Keith. In no time they translated the dishes described in curlicued writing.

Keith snapped his fingers in an imperious gesture. *"Garçon!"* He rattled off a sentence in French.

Jackie giggled. "You just asked for something for your travel sickness."

He smacked his forehead in mock dismay. "Oh, yeah. I'm supposed to order that *after* dinner." He looked at her. "Are you going with us to Le Provençal?"

"I don't know. Mr. McConnell wants me to. He said it would be good experience."

"You ought to come," he said. "It'll be cool."

"Well — " She hesitated.

"Just say yes." Keith supplied the word. *"Sí."*

She laughed. "That's Spanish!"

Mr. McConnell collected the menus. "Well, Jackie? Will you join us on our field trip?"

"I'd like to," she replied. An evening with Keith would be fun, in any language.

The next day, when she told her friends about the meeting, they responded to her news with enthusiasm.

"Jackie!" Carol shrieked. "This is practically a *date*. Going to a romantic French restaurant with a boy!"

"And eight other people plus a teacher," Jackie said dryly.

"But you'll be on that long bus ride together and then at the restaurant. . . ." Frieda rolled her eyes. "You've never had a French meal before. They go on for *hours*. That's all people in France do is eat."

"You have to wear just the right outfit," Paula put in. "Not too dressy but elegant. And heels. Definitely heels."

"I don't have any heels," Jackie said. "Or an elegant dress." But their excitement was contagious. It really *was* almost a date. *Any*thing could happen between appetizers and dessert in a romantic French restaurant.

Frieda became her usual take-charge self. "We have to help Jackie find the perfect dress. We could all go shopping together."

"I have a pair of genuine ruby earrings you could borrow," Carol offered. "They're just little stones but they're real. They came with a set my father got my mother, only she doesn't have pierced ears so she gave them to me."

A shopping trip, ruby earrings! Her friends were so generous and not the least bit jealous that she was going out with a boy (and nine other people). Jackie didn't speak for a second and then Frieda said, "You're the first in our group to go out. When it's our turn, you can do the same for us."

Life was so much easier, Jackie discovered, when you're a part of the bunch, instead of constantly striving to be at the top. Her sister Sharon could learn a lot from her friends.

Her mother took her shopping to buy heels. Jackie wobbled around the thickly carpeted store in black patent leather pumps with little rosettes on the toes, twisting her ankles like pretzels.

"You'll get the hang of walking in them," her mother said. "It just takes practice. Those shoes look darling on your feet."

At home, Jackie stalked around the kitchen in her new shoes and a pair of her mother's pantyhose. She practiced walking and sitting and crossing her legs to show off her darling feet.

Her mother came in with the mail. "There's something here from the college," she said, slitting a creamy envelope. "I wonder what it is."

"Maybe Sharon's in trouble," Jackie suggested hopefully. She still hadn't forgiven her sister and she never would. Not ever.

"She made the Dean's list," Mrs. Howard crowed. Then her face fell. "But there's a mistake."

"I believe it." Jackie tottered over on her high heels. "Sharon never made good grades before."

"No, I mean the letter is for someone else." She showed it to Jackie. "See? It's for Sharon Leigh."

Jackie stared at the letter. "Maybe Sharon changed her name so she could get on the Dean's list."

"Don't be ridiculous."

"No, it's possible." With Sharon, anything was possible. "Remember the time she forged your comments on her report card?" Jackie pitched her voice higher, pretending to be a younger version of her sister. " 'I am glad Sharon is doing better.' "

"That was back in elementary school," Mrs. Howard said, as if that made forgery okay. "She only wrote a few words and we caught her the next time report cards came out. Jackie, this isn't the same thing. Sharon's in college now. She can't fake letters from the dean's office. I'm going to clear this up right now." Her mother headed for the telephone in the hall.

Jackie headed for her room. She didn't even want to hear anybody talking to her sister the creep, much less speak to her herself. Sharon never answered Jackie's venomous letter, but Jackie didn't care. If she never saw her sister again, it would be too soon.

A few moments later her mother came into her room. "She changed her name," she announced, incredulous. "The letter was no mistake."

Despite her resolution not to care about anything her sister did, Jackie asked, "She changed her name? Just like that?"

Her mother nodded. "From Margie Sharon Howard to Sharon Leigh. She said she always hated the name Margie because it was so old-fashioned. When she gets out to Hollywood, Sharon Leigh will sound better. Did you ever hear such nonsense? Sometimes I think that girl's lost her marbles."

"How did she change it? I mean, did she go to court or something?"

"She just did it! The way Sharon does everything, on impulse. Of course it isn't legal. She went into the office at school and told them her papers were wrong and that she'd just noticed it. Somehow she bamboozled the secretary into changing her name on her records. She says she's sent away for a new driver's license, too, using her college papers as proof. This will cause her legal problems for years and years. You can't just arbitrarily change your name because you don't like it."

Jackie had known lots of kids who hated their names, like Clarence DeBell and Stedman Arnold. She didn't mind her own name, but she felt sorry for kids who had gotten stuck with clunkers. She often thought kids should be given a temporary name at birth and then be allowed to change it when they were old enough to pick out one they liked.

"Sharon Leigh," Jackie recited. Her sister had always been Margie Sharon Howard, even though no one ever used her first name.

"Wait'll your father hears this," Mrs. Howard said. "He's going to hit the roof. If it's not one thing with that girl, it's another."

Jackie's trip to the French restaurant and her new high heels receded from importance as Sharon's latest problem leaped to the foreground. Her parents would undoubtedly discuss this new development endlessly.

"But Sharon made the Dean's list," Jackie pointed out. In the distress over the changed name, Sharon's achievement had been forgotten.

"Yes, she did," her mother said with a sigh.

"And I told her we were delighted about that, but why did she have to ruin things by changing her name?"

Because, Jackie wanted to tell her, Sharon wasn't really *happy* unless she was in the limelight. Being on the Dean's list wasn't enough for Sharon — she had to do something drastic besides, like changing her name.

Jackie was glad her name was Jacqueline Howard. She wouldn't have traded places with Margie Sharon Leigh Howard for anything.

Chapter 12

Jackie circled the day of the French Club dinner in red on the kitchen calendar, pleased that she, too, had an important occasion to mark so she wouldn't forget. As if she could. Hanging in her closet was a new blue-flowered spring dress, elegant but not too fancy, and the new shoes with heels. She had Carol's ruby earrings, a purse from Paula that matched her shoes, and lots of advice from Frieda. Jackie almost felt like a bride with the requisite something old, something new, something borrowed, something blue.

Mr. McConnell — since she had met Keith, Jackie no longer thought of him as Adair — outlined the agenda for the trip in minute detail at a special French Club meeting. The club would assemble in his classroom after school. They would take a bus downtown to the restaurant. Jackie thought that driving to a fancy place like Le Provençal in a yellow school bus was rather tacky, but the club couldn't afford to hire a limo. Because they were eating early on a Tuesday evening, a private dining room would be made available to them. They would have dinner, get back on the bus, and drive back to Virginia to Fairfax High, where their parents would pick them up.

On Monday afternoon, the day before the big dinner, Jackie checked her outfit once more. Everything was perfect. Tomorrow she would wear her new dress to school. She planned to carry the high heels in a tote bag — walking around school all day on stilts was too much. Kids would probably tease the members of the French Club since they would all be too dressed up for an ordinary school day, but it would be good-natured kidding, maybe mingled with a little envy.

Jackie sat down on the floor to change purses, a ritual she had watched her mother do many times. She dumped junk out of her shapeless everyday purse and selected the essentials she needed for one evening: a pen, a small brush and mirror, lip gloss, tissues, a tiny tube of hand lotion, and her emergency cash. The dinner was already paid for, but her mother insisted she take along extra money. She tucked these items into Paula's rectangular clutch bag.

She would be like those women who strode around Washington, D.C., in high heels, carrying a small purse. Freed from the burden of schoolbooks and a weighty purse, Jackie would be her own person! Someone smart and confident, someone who could order a meal in French. This was going to be more than a dinner. At last the real Jacqueline Howard would be unveiled.

She took her diary from the vanity drawer, eager to write down her latest revelation. The phone rang.

"I'll get it," Jackie called, running from her room. "It's probably Frieda."

But Mrs. Howard reached the phone first. "Sharon!" she said, her face lighting up. Jackie turned to go back to her room when she heard her mother say, after a long pause, "You'd better tell her yourself. She's right here."

"I don't want to talk to her! I'm still mad at her!"

Apparently Sharon was going on and on about something because her mother listened before she finally said, "All right. We'll talk about it then." Mrs. Howard hung up and looked at Jackie.

"Whatever Sharon said, I'm not interested, so don't bother to tell me," Jackie said.

"She's on her way home," Mrs. Howard told her, ignoring her request. "Tomorrow she's scheduled to take her state board exams in Richmond and the lady who was supposed to be her model can't go. She's sick or something, so Sharon is coming to get you."

At first Jackie didn't understand. Then the

meaning struck her with full force. "I can't go to Richmond tomorrow — I'm going to my French Club dinner downtown!"

"I know. She was so frantic I didn't have a chance to tell her. The girl who was bringing her home was beeping the horn outside. Evidently Sharon just found out the woman canceled, and she barely had time to make new arrangements."

"What arrangements?" Jackie demanded. "Did she *ask* me if I wanted to go to Richmond? No, she just said she was coming to get me. Well, I'm not going and that's that!"

"She'll be here in a couple of hours. You can discuss it with her then." Her mother went out to the kitchen to start supper.

Jackie stormed back to her room. Her borrowed purse, her new dress, the shoes, the ruby earrings . . . everything was waiting for her to make her debut as her own person tomorrow. She would *not* let her sister ruin it for her.

Sharon's ride didn't pull up in the driveway until after they had eaten supper and Jackie and Mrs. Howard were washing the dishes.

Sharon scuffed into the house, lugging a tote bag of hairstyling equipment and a paper bag with her overnight things. Her sister's appearance stunned Jackie. Sharon's hair, still short and dyed her natural color, was stuffed into an unattractive scarf. Her face was drawn. The black smudges under her eyes were not from smeared mascara, but from lack of sleep. She wore a wrinkled blouse over old pants, like someone who had dressed hurriedly in the middle of the night after a fire alarm went off.

"I'm here," she said wearily, setting her bags on the floor to receive her mother's hug.

"Big deal," Jackie muttered, throwing the tea towel on the counter. The Great One had arrived, now everyone would bow and scrape the way they always did whenever Sharon barged into their lives.

"You're too thin," Mrs. Howard declared. "I've got a plate for you in the oven. I know you haven't eaten."

"Thanks, Mom. Hi, Dad." Sharon kissed her father, who was reading the paper at the table. Then she sank into the chair opposite him with her chin in her hands. "It feels so good to be home."

Sharon didn't seem to notice Jackie, and Jackie wasn't about to greet her sister, not even when her mother told her to take Sharon's plate to her.

Sharon looked up as Jackie set the warm plate down. "Hey, Bony Maronie. Are you all ready for tomorrow?"

"If you're referring to that business about Richmond, you'll have to find somebody else," Jackie said stiffly. "I have other plans."

"What are you talking about?" Sharon held her fork loosely as if too exhausted to eat. "Mom, what's she talking about?"

Mrs. Howard assumed the neutral expression she used whenever the girls got into a fight. "You'd better ask Jackie, Sharon. This is between you two."

Sharon caught Jackie's wrist. "Tell me what you're talking about. I'm too tired to play games."

"I'm going out to dinner tomorrow night." Jackie pulled her wrist free. "Downtown. To Le Provençal, with the French Club. The menus are written entirely in French and the waiters only speak French, so we — "

Sharon interrupted, "I *need* you to go to Richmond with me!"

"Will we be back by five?" Jackie inquired.

"Of course not. The test is a full day."

"Then I can't make it. Sorry."

"You *have* to go with me!" her sister cried desperately. "I don't have anyone else, and I'm scheduled to take my boards at nine o'clock. I don't have time to find another model."

"You should have thought of that a few months ago when you decided your landlady had better hair than mine," Jackie said haughtily, amazed her mother hadn't stepped in by now to order Jackie to go.

"She does have better hair. It's going gray and it's thicker than yours. But she came down with bursitis in her hip yesterday, and she told me she couldn't stand that long drive and all those hours in the chair."

"Well, that's the breaks. If you'll excuse me," Jackie said with elaborate politeness, "I need to get my beauty sleep so I'll be refreshed for my dinner appointment tomorrow." She patted back a yawn.

"Jackie!" Sharon said. "I have worked double

shifts for *months* to get my hours in and keep up my grades. If I miss the board exam tomorrow, I can't take it again until they reschedule it in the fall."

"I don't care if you've worked triple shifts," Jackie yelled. "You think you can treat me any old way — tell me one minute you want me to go, the next you don't. Now you're in trouble, and you think you can come home and get good old Jackie to fill in!" She would not give up her dinner just because her sister snapped her fingers. Margie Sharon Leigh Howard would find out that Jacqueline Howard was no pushover.

"Girls!" Mrs. Howard held her palm up like a referee. "No screaming. We'll settle this civilly. Sharon, it is obvious you have worked very hard and we understand your predicament, but you really shouldn't expect Jackie to drop everything and run when you come home. She *does* have other plans, and you should respect that."

Jackie's mouth opened in surprise. Her mother was actually standing up to Sharon, in defense of Jackie!

Sharon stared at her mother. "I can't believe I'm hearing this! You're putting her stupid dinner before my STATE BOARD EXAMS! *A freshman club meeting before my whole life!*"

"I'm not putting Jackie's plans before your exams," Mrs. Howard clarified. "I'm saying you should respect your sister's plans. She has a life, too. Jackie, I know how much this dinner means to you. You bought a new dress and new shoes and everything. But your sister is in a terrible bind. She needs your help tomorrow."

Sharon sagged in her chair. "Please," she said to Jackie. "Will you help me just this once? Will you go with me to Richmond and be my model?"

"You don't want *me*," Jackie accused. "You just want my *hair*. Any dummy will do as long as its got hair!"

"What do you want me to do, get on my knees and beg?" Sharon said. And then, amazingly, she began to cry.

Jackie stared at her sister, shaken. Sharon hardly *ever* cried, unlike Jackie, who had earned the nickname "Waterworks" over the years. Either Sharon was closer to exhaustion than their mother implied, or this trip meant the world and all to her.

"I can't make you go," Sharon sobbed. "I can only ask. Jackie, will you go with me to Richmond tomorrow?"

Her sister didn't look like her usual beautiful, sophisticated, charge-ahead self. She looked small in her baggy clothes, and frightened. Pathetic, even.

Jackie wanted desperately to go to the dinner, to be her own person. But having her sister bawling and groveling at her feet was a totally new experience. She wasn't a selfish pig — she realized the importance of Sharon's test. A club dinner couldn't be compared to a state board exam.

"Whatever you decide," Mr. Howard said to Jackie, "is all right with us. Just think it over carefully." To Sharon he added, "I want you to know that your mother and I were never crazy about the idea of your taking Jackie all the way to Richmond for your test. But if Jackie agrees to go, we'll help any way we can. I'll run up to Centreville and get gas for the car tonight, so you'll be ready to leave first thing."

"All the gas in Saudi Arabia won't do me any good if I don't have a model," Sharon snuffled. "If you didn't want Jackie to go with me, why didn't you say something at Christmas?"

Mrs. Howard put one arm around Sharon and smoothed Jackie's long hair with her free hand. "Because Jackie is old enough to make her own decisions. I can't keep her here forever, any more than I could keep you at home. But I do need her . . . she's my baby."

Her mother was afraid to send both her daughters out into the world, Jackie realized, startled. Jackie knew her mother loved her, too, even while she fretted over Sharon. Her mother was okay, really. She remembered giggling in the shoe store the other day — her mother was almost as excited as Jackie over Jackie's first pair of high heels. And her mother didn't yell at her for eating all the buttermints.

It must be hard, Jackie thought, putting herself in her mother's place for a second, to have children around for years and then have them leave. She knew how bad *she* felt when Sharon had left. Jackie forgave her mother for the unbronzed walking shoes and the paperback baby book.

Jackie squeezed her mother around the waist. "It's all right, Mama. We're only going to Richmond. We'll be back tomorrow evening."

Sharon smiled through her tears. "Oh, Jackie, thank you! You're saving my life!" She did everything but kiss Jackie's hand.

"I'm going," Jackie qualified briskly, "because your exam is too important to miss. But I don't like it one bit. What time do we have to get up in the morning?"

Sharon calculated on her fingers. "We have to be there at nine . . . it's a two-hour drive. Say, a half an hour to find the place and park . . . we ought to be on the road no later than five-thirty, just to be on the safe side. We can stop and eat breakfast someplace."

"I'll be in the car at five-thirty." Without another word, Jackie flounced off to her room.

The sight of the blue-flowered dress and her new shoes made her want to cry. *Again* Sharon had managed to wreck her life! Would she *ever* be free of her sister, free to become her own person?

She undressed, slipped into her nightgown, and got into bed. A short time later she heard her sister trudge into the bathroom, run water, then come out, pausing by Jackie's door.

"Jackie?" Sharon said tentatively. " 'Night. See you in the morning."

Jackie turned her face stonily to the wall and closed her eyes until her sister went into the guest room. Just because she was going didn't mean she was going to act all nicey-nicey. When she opened her eyes again, the pale light of early morning lay in stripes across her bed. Sharon was stirring around in the next room.

Jackie got dressed and went out to the kitchen. Her parents were having coffee.

"I'll call your French teacher and explain that you had to go out of town and can't make the dinner tonight," her mother said.

"Is that what you're going to tell him? That I had to go out of town?" She liked the phrase — it made her sound as if she were a globe-trotter, staying home only long enough to wash her clothes and read her messages before zipping out of town again.

Sharon appeared in the doorway, her tote bag slung over one shoulder. "I guess we'd better get moving, Jackie. See you folks tonight. Wish me luck!"

Outside, dew lay heavily on the grass. In the woods behind the house, a mockingbird tested his stamina, and their early-morning nerves, with a rollicking song.

"Drive carefully," Mr. Howard warned Sharon. "Keep your speed down and watch out for the truckers."

"I will," Sharon promised. She put the car in gear and backed out of the driveway. "I hope I can remember how to get there," she told Jackie as they headed south for Interstate 95. "My instructor wrote down directions. We just stay on 95 until we get to Richmond. Then we have to go to the John Marshall Hotel."

Jackie stared out the window at the dull scenery. So far she had not spoken a single word to her sister. Sharon might have won, but Jackie did not have to pretend she was having a good time when she wasn't. Nowhere in Sharon's rulebook was there anything about hair models being required to talk. All Sharon wanted was a dummy to work on, and that was what she was getting.

Chapter 13

They stopped at Aunt Sarah's Pancake House in Fredericksburg for breakfast. Jackie ordered French toast, the closest she'd get to a French meal, she figured, while Sharon ordered only black coffee and a muffin, which she didn't eat.

"Are you going to not talk to me the entire day or what?" Sharon demanded.

Jackie drizzled syrup over her French toast so slowly the syrup poured out of the bottle in a thin, spider-web strand. "I never said I wasn't talking to you. I just don't have anything to say, that's all." With her knife and fork, she cut her toast into neat squares.

"For heaven's sake, we're not at a Sunday school picnic. Eat faster!"

"If I eat too fast, I'll get carsick." Jackie chewed

a bite methodically. She decided that answering Sharon's direct questions and making noncommital remarks like "pass the salt" did not count as real conversation.

"You're going to be sick all over if you don't hurry up," Sharon warned. "We have a long drive ahead of us. We're only a third of the way there."

Jackie finished her meal quickly, staring out the fly-specked window instead of at her sister, who monitored every single bite she took.

When they were back in the car, Sharon flipped her blue beauty school textbook across the seat toward Jackie. "Would you quiz me? I don't know which I'm the most nervous about, the written part of the exam or the demonstration."

Since asking questions fell into the same category as answering questions, and therefore did not constitute real conversation, Jackie opened the book.

"Do that skin chart first," Sharon said.

Jackie located the chart. "Name the parts of the skin."

Drumming her fingers on the steering wheel, Sharon chanted, "Subcutaneous fat, the dermis, the epidermis. Around the hair follicle is the sebaceous gland. There are also sweat glands, capillary vessels, and — uh, pores."

"You forgot the scaly layer," Jackie said smugly. It was wonderful to tell her sister she was wrong.

"Go on with the questions."

"What is acne rosacea?" Jackie stumbled over the pronunciation.

"Rosacea is a chronic facial problem which produces pimples, pustules, and . . . redness in the central part of the face."

Jackie felt her sticky French toast turn over in her uneasy stomach. Would all the skin questions be that gross? "Name the three stages of dermatitis."

"Acute, subacute, and chronic," Sharon replied instantly.

"What is the difference between dermatitis and eczema?"

"None. They are both the same skin disorder."

Jackie was wearying of skin problems before seven in the morning, especially on a full stomach. The photographs illustrating each definition made Jackie even queasier. She closed the book. "I don't feel so good."

Sharon ripped her gaze from the road to throw Jackie a horrified glance. "You're not getting sick, are you? So help me, Jackie — "

"It's reading while the car is in motion," Jackie said, quoting her mother. Car sickness was not new with her. She used to get sick while reading highway signs and often would have to crawl into the front seat to sit between her parents while Sharon, alone in the back seat, muttered caustic remarks about the precious little baby and her weak stomach.

"Well, put the book away then," Sharon said. "I guess I know the material by now. I've studied it enough."

They rode a while in silence. Interstate 95, Jackie discovered, was unbelievably boring. There was nothing to look at except billboards advertising Stuckey's pecan pralines and an endless monotony of pine trees. Her first trip anywhere in her life and it was proving to be boring as dishwater.

"Mom said you got new high heels the other day," Sharon said amiably. "What color?"

"Black." The shoes reminded Jackie of the dinner she was missing. Of course her inconsiderate sister wouldn't think of that. Sharon only thought of herself.

"Is the heel very high?" Sharon pursued.

"No."

"What about straps? Do they have straps?"

"No."

Her sister heaved a sigh. "Don't hurt yourself answering."

"I'm not."

"All right," Sharon said crisply. "If you want to be that way . . . I'm not going to waste my breath talking to you."

She concentrated on the road, and Jackie went back to the scenery. They drove in mutual silence for more than an hour, until the traffic began to get heavy, an indication they were approaching the city.

Sharon hunched over the wheel, as she searched for the right exit off the interstate. "Do you suppose you can help me find the hotel?" she asked tartly. "If it's not too much trouble? We're looking for the John Marshall Hotel."

148

They cruised down Broad Street, blending with commuters who worked in the city. Jackie was disappointed with Richmond, once the capital of the Confederacy. She expected to see plantation houses and flowering magnolias, but there were only modern buildings and sidewalks.

"There it is!" she shouted, seeing the hotel on the corner. "The John Marshall Hotel, right there."

"Great. Now if we can just find a place to park." Sharon drove up and down side streets until she found a slot. For all her early practice in the driveway when she was Jackie's age, Sharon was not a very good parallel parker. She backed and filled and pulled in and out of the space until a construction worker took pity on her and guided her into the slot. Red-faced, Sharon thanked him.

She reached into the back seat for her tote bag and purse. "Okay," she told Jackie. "Let's go. The doors close at nine o'clock on the dot. We've got ten minutes to hike down to the hotel."

They practically ran the distance. Jackie had a hard time keeping up with her sister, who had longer legs. She gulped in too much air and got the hiccups.

She entered the gracious lobby of the huge hotel, hiccuping loudly as Sharon asked for directions to the ballroom.

"Stop that!" Sharon hissed. "Everybody's looking at you. You don't hiccup in a place like the John Marshall." She spoke of the hotel as if she frequented it every other weekend.

149

Jackie tried to will her hiccups away as she gawked at the surroundings. The lobby of the hotel was beautiful, with high ceilings and velvet-covered furniture and lush potted plants. A perfect place to relax while Sharon was taking her written exam and meet a handsome southern boy. Maybe the trip wouldn't be a total loss after all.

Sharon hustled her down a long carpeted corridor. "Jackie, will you *hurry*?" She was so nervous, her voice quavered.

"You're going to register or whatever and then take your written test, right?" Jackie asked, her mind still on southern boys.

"I suppose. Why?"

"Because I want to sit out in the lobby. The hair people probably won't let the models in that room anyway. Afraid we might slip you the answers or something."

"I don't care," Sharon said. "Just so you're around when I need you."

At the entrance to the ballroom, they were pushed inside by anxious students and their models crowding the double doors. Jackie gasped and grabbed the back of Sharon's blouse. Hundreds of people crammed into the enormous ballroom.

They just made it. Precisely at nine o'clock, according to the big clock set up on a table, two men closed the double doors with the finality of sealing them in a dungeon. Another man with a microphone called the room to order, no small task. Then he began to call attendance. As each name was called, the trainee and her model stepped to the other side of the room.

Sharon fidgeted, worried that her name would not be on the list. "My instructor sent my name down here along with the other girls who were ready. I should be on the list but you never can tell — " When the man called her name, she hollered, "Here!" and towed Jackie to the other side of the room with her.

"All these people were in your school?" Jackie marveled.

"Are you kidding? Everybody from the entire state is here," Sharon replied. "I don't see the other girls from my school. I doubt I ever will in this mob."

After the lengthy roll was called, the man explained the procedure. Because of the size of the crowd, they would begin demonstrations immediately and while the models were under the dryers, the trainees would take their written exams. Jackie winced inwardly. So much for her plan to enchant some handsome southern boy in the luxurious lobby.

The trainees were put into sections and were sent to the restrooms to wet their models' hair. Sharon was in the second section but waiting for the first group to get back was an eternity. "We will be here all night at the rate people are moving," she complained. When the first group returned with wet-haired models, she dragged Jackie to the front of her section, collecting glares from other girls.

The restroom had seven sinks. Lines formed

behind the sinks and into the stalls.

"This is ridiculous," Sharon fumed. "They should have better facilities." She practically drowned Jackie in her nervousness as she wet Jackie's hair under the faucet. Jackie whacked her head on the faucet handle as she came up for air, spluttering.

Back in the ballroom, they were assigned a station. In it was a straight chair instead of the pneumatic chairs Sharon was accustomed to, a table, a dinky mirror, and a paper bag.

"Look, they've given you your very own barf bag," Jackie said.

On the table was a tall bottle of disinfectant for cleaning brushes and combs that fell on the floor. Sharon spilled the equipment from her tote bag onto the table. An assistant handed her a plastic cape.

"Sit down," Sharon told Jackie. She swathed her in the cape and tied the neck strings good and tight with trembling hands.

Jackie ran her finger around the band, trying to loosen it a bit. She wondered if she would live to see the end of this test. It was very hot in the room with so many anxious sweating girls and the plastic cape, which fell below her knees, was like being enveloped in Saran wrap.

"I have to cut your hair first," Sharon said.

"Cut my hair! You never said anything about cutting my hair!" Jackie declared.

"I *have* to. I have to demonstrate scissor-over-comb technique. It's part of the test." Sharon looked worried, as if expecting Jackie to spring up out of the chair. "I thought you knew that," she added in a small voice.

"What else didn't you tell me?" Jackie said in an accusing tone. "Okay, but not too much. I've been growing my hair for a year, you know."

"I won't, I won't," her sister promised hastily. "I'll just trim it. You've got split ends anyway."

Sharon listened intensely to the assistant who explained the hair cut procedure. She had fifteen minutes to perform the cut. The paper bag was supposed to be fastened to the back of the chair and each piece of hair dropped into it. She could not drop a single hair on the floor, she was cautioned, or she'd be marked down.

"You can't cut hair and catch it at the same time!" Sharon protested.

"I know," the girl next to her said, swiping at her model's hair with a comb. "It's a stupid rule. They just don't want to sweep hair." She smiled at Sharon. "I'm Reba, from Lynchburg. Where are you from?"

"I'm Sharon, from Fairfax," Sharon replied, combing Jackie's hair with uneven jerks. Jackie's head snapped like a rubber band.

"Oh, the fancy part of the state."

Jackie gaped at the other girl in amazement. Did other people actually think where they lived was grand, like the lobby of the John Marshall Hotel?

"This is my mother. Mrs. Weber," Reba went on. The woman in her chair waved.

"Nice to meet you. This is my sister," was all Sharon said.

153

"Doesn't she have long pretty hair?" Reba remarked, smiling at Jackie. Jackie smiled back. People always said that about Sharon's hair, but never hers.

"Sharon's just going to trim it," she told Reba. "I've been growing my hair for a whole year."

Sharon danced around Jackie's chair, stretching out a lock of hair, cutting it and catching it all at the same time. The mirror was turned away from Jackie so she couldn't see her sister's face, but she imagined it was very tense. She watched Reba, who kept dropping first her scissors, then her comb.

"Whoops," Mrs. Weber said every time her daughter dropped something. "You've got butterfingers today."

Once Sharon bent close to Jackie's ear. "That girl doesn't even know how to hold a comb," she whispered. "She'll never pass."

If the judges were as strict as the trainees around them were lamenting, Sharon was probably right. Armed with clipboards and serious frowns, they roamed around the stations, mutely checking haircutting techniques. Jackie decided Mr. Revlon wouldn't be caught dead in a place like this.

"I'm done," Sharon said. "But that judge will take forever to get over here." She spritzed Jackie's hair with a spray bottle. "If your hair's too dry, he won't be able to see the lines of the cut."

Jackie was afraid to move her head but her neck felt awfully — bare. She had no idea how

154

much Sharon had cut off, since all the hair was dropped in the bag pinned to the back of the chair.

"How much did you cut off?" she asked Sharon.

Sharon was busily signaling the roving judge. "I had to give you a regulation haircut," she hedged. "They changed the rules on me here."

"HOW MUCH?"

Suddenly Reba turned from her mother and shrieked. "Oh, my goodness, you didn't have to chop off all that child's hair!"

Jackie seized the mirror. Sharon had cut her hair, her long beautiful hair that took a whole year to grow, up to her chin! She started to cry, loud, gulping sobs.

"Jackie, don't do this to me," Sharon said, wringing her hands. "I'm sorry I had to cut so much, but the rules said a quarter of an inch from the nape — "

"Not that much," said Reba. "*Two inches* from the nape." She went back to her mother and snipped a big chunk of hair from over the woman's ear.

"You cut off my hair!" Jackie wailed. "I've been growing it for a whole year and you just chopped it off!"

"Jackie, don't make a scene," Sharon pleaded. "I guess I misread the rule sheet. I'll make it up to you, I promise. When we get out of here, I'll give you the cutest — "

But Jackie didn't want to hear another false

promise from her sister. She leaped off the chair and ran through the ballroom, winding her way between chairs.

She burst through the first door she came to, blinded by her tears and the bright sunlight outside.

The door led to a parking lot. Jackie ran between the parked cars, sobbing, her plastic cape flying behind her.

Chapter 14

Jackie halted by a station wagon, her breath coming in choking gasps. She caught a glimpse of herself in the side-view mirror. She looked like a shorn sheep! How could Sharon do this to her, knowing that Jackie's hair was her pride and joy? She hated Sharon! Hated her!

She didn't know what she was going to do, but she was *not* going back into that ballroom. Let her sister find another victim.

"Jackie!" Sharon pelted between the rows of cars, still carrying her comb and scissors. "What are you doing out here? You scared me to death."

"Go away." Jackie doggedly walked in the other direction, the plastic cape dragging limply from the neckband. In her flight, the cape had somehow spun around and hung down her back.

157

"Jackie, you have to come back." Sharon jogged alongside her. "The judges haven't even graded my haircut. They saw you run out and they stopped the clock for me, but they won't wait forever."

"So tell somebody who cares." Jackie didn't slacken her pace. They were almost out of the parking lot.

Sharon clutched her arm, forcing her to stop by the dumpsters, which were prettily disguised by a row of maple trees. "Listen, I'm sorry about the haircut — I really am. Jackie, I was so nervous, I got the directions confused. When we get back home, I'll give you a really cute haircut. You've got a small face, you'd look darling in a short, feathered cut — "

"I don't want short hair!" Jackie bellowed. "I want my long hair! You did it on purpose!"

"What do you want me to *do*? I can't put it back on your head," Sharon cried. Beads of perspiration glimmered on her upper lip. "I'll do anything you ask if you'll come back inside with me. Whatever you want, you can have. Just name it."

Jackie pondered the possibilities. She could ask for anything. Anything! Why, she could ask for Sharon's cat . . . or the twenty dollar bill corner Sharon carried in her wallet for good luck.

But then she realized she would only be holding Sharon's cherished possessions hostage. They wouldn't belong to her. The bill corner wouldn't bring Jackie luck and nobody owned a cat, really. And they wouldn't make up for having her hair cut off.

If only they could go back to the days when life was simpler. Suddenly, Jackie wanted Sharon to lift her up and do the trick they used to do when they were younger. She wanted her sister to spin her around and around until she was giggling and dizzy. But the last time they tried the trick, they discovered Jackie's legs were too long and her feet wouldn't clear the ground. It was funny, but it was sad, too. They had outgrown part of their shared past. Maybe, she thought now, they had outgrown each other as well.

"Jackie," Sharon begged. "Please come back with me. If I don't, the judges will automatically flunk me, and I won't be able to retake the test until next fall. I have to get my career going, don't you see?"

"I see you want to be Sharon of Hollywood," Jackie said bitterly. "What does that make me?"

Sharon stared at her, puzzled.

Jackie knew she wasn't making much sense, but she waited for Sharon's reply. If Sharon said "my little sister," Jackie would start walking toward Interstate 95.

"Well, that doesn't make you anything besides what you are," Sharon said slowly. "Yourself. Jacqueline Howard."

"And not you," Jackie said.

"Of course not me," Sharon said. "How can you be me? You're your own person. And I'm my own person. We are two separate people. Will you come back with me so I can finish my test?"

What else could she do, hang around the dumpsters all day? Her hair was in the bag clipped to the back of the chair. Nothing or no one could fix it now. "Yes," she sighed.

Inside, Sharon rewet Jackie's hair in the drinking fountain in the lobby.

"I thought you said we were supposed to act proper in a fancy place like this," Jackie said.

"I'm not about to stand in that line in the bathroom again," Sharon declared, taking charge once more.

The scene in the ballroom was utter chaos. Girls sobbed over ruined haircuts, screaming that the judges were unfair or too slow. One girl screeched at her model, "Why did you give yourself a perm? I can't get a comb through your hair!" The model replied timidly, "I just wanted to look nice." Another girl threw up in her purse. Jackie wondered why she didn't use the paper bag clipped to the back of the chair. As she and Sharon got in line to have Sharon's haircut graded, a girl in another line swayed on her feet, then slumped to the floor. Jackie imagined they'd send the girl to the clinic, where she'd have to lie on a paper-blanketed cot all day guarded by an eagle-eyed nurse who had no sympathy for fakers.

"Now for the set," Sharon said, as she led Jackie back to her station. She wet Jackie's hair yet again with the spray bottle, then began sectioning it off.

"I see your sister came back," Reba said to Sharon. She was twisting her mother's hair into tortured-looking curls.

"We had a little misunderstanding." Sharon worked quickly, pushing Jackie's hair into fingerwaves at the crown which she secured with clips, then began on the rollers.

"Is it three rollers on the top and then the perm rods?" Reba asked Sharon.

"Three rollers. Full-base, half-base, no base," Sharon replied. Her fingers felt efficient in Jackie's hair, not fumbling like Reba's. Her sister was going to pass this exam, Jackie decided.

"I wish I'd stayed in Lynchburg," Reba moaned. "I can get a job in the drugstore."

"You'll do just fine," Reba's mother assured her. She winced as her daughter yanked a strand of hair. "Mrs. Graham is keeping a place open in her shop."

Sharon moved in front of Jackie to work on her bangs. Their eyes met briefly. Jackie knew from Sharon's expression that Reba didn't have a chance. She hoped the judges wouldn't be too hard on Reba.

A judge came by to check Sharon's technique. Then he told her her model could be put under the dryer and she could take the written exam. Jackie was herded over to a row of dryers. Sharon set the timer, then ran off to the exam room.

161

Just as Jackie was about to pass out from the blowing heat, Sharon returned, her face pinched with tension. She raised the bonnet so Jackie could stagger out.

"We have a fifteen-minute lunch break," she announced. "They've got sandwiches and drinks set up next door."

Like every other aspect of the day, the lunch room was quickly disintegrating to riot status. Jackie saw immediately that there wasn't enough food, much less enough time to eat it. She wormed through the crowd to the tables and grabbed sandwiches and two miniature bags of potato chips, while Sharon fought for two cans of soda. They camped on the floor by the wall, placing their lunch in the protective circle made by their legs.

"What is this?" Sharon peeled the top piece of bread off her sandwich and made a horrible face. "Liverwurst. Ugh! What've you got?"

Jackie's wasn't much better, ham salad. They divided their sandwiches between them, sharing the good with the bad. When Jackie said she was still hungry, Sharon bravely attacked the food tables to get her another bag of potato chips.

Back at Sharon's station, Sharon began the comb-out, a meticulous process that made Jackie's neck ache from holding her head erect.

Next to them, Reba and her mother were arguing because Reba had put disinfectant on her mother's hair instead of the pretend permanent solution the trainees were supposed to dab on the perm rods. Mrs. Weber had a big orange spot right in the middle of her head. Jackie was glad Sharon didn't get the bottles switched. It was bad enough Sharon scalped her, but an orange spot would have been the last straw.

Once more, Jackie and Sharon waited in a long line for the judge to examine Sharon's comb-out. The woman tilted Jackie's head this way and that, as if her head was mounted on ballbearings, then made meaningless squiggles on her clipboard. She didn't say a word to Sharon.

"That's it," Sharon said, weaving back to her station. "We can go home." She tossed equipment into her tote bag while Jackie stared at her dreadful hairstyle in the mirror. "You want me to comb those curls out?" Sharon offered. "It won't take a second."

"No." She could live with the awful hairstyle if it meant getting home sooner.

Sharon glanced over at Reba's empty station. "I wanted to say good-bye to her and her mother, but I guess they've gone. Okay, let's go, too."

They were silent as they walked through the lavish lobby and up the street to the car. Jackie leaned her head against the window as Sharon maneuvered the car through city rush-hour traffic to the interstate. She fell into an exhausted sleep, with her head rolling against the pane of glass.

She woke up when she sensed the car slowing down. They were driving off an exit ramp.

"Supper time," Sharon said. "I feel like I haven't eaten in weeks. You can find something

163

at Aunt Sarah's Pancake House, can't you?"

"Are we in Fredericksburg already?" Jackie sat up. They were in front of the restaurant for the second time that day. Jackie felt weird, as if she had dreamed the events in the John Marshall Hotel.

Sharon got out and stretched. "You should see your hair. It's all flat on one side."

"It's also about a foot too short," Jackie grumbled. Her mouth felt tinny inside. She hated to sleep in the middle of the day.

After they ordered, Sharon said, "I told you I was sorry and I am. I feel awful." She buried her face in her hands, rubbing her forehead. "What a day."

Jackie fiddled with the sugar shaker, lifting the little silver flap. "How come they didn't tell you if you passed or not?"

"They just don't. I'll be notified by mail, in about a month."

"I think that's mean."

"I think so, too. I planned to start working this summer. At this shop in Harrisonburg. I hope they let me know before the lady hires somebody else."

Their food came then. When the waitress left, Jackie said, "Then you won't be coming home this summer?"

"No. I already mentioned this to Mom and Dad."

Jackie scraped the seeds off her hamburger bun with her fork and laid them on the edge of her plate. Sharon wasn't coming home for the summer. That meant Sharon had left home for good.

"If you're not coming back," Jackie said, "I guess I can say Felix is my cat."

Sharon paused, her hamburger in one hand, and considered. "I guess you're right. My landlady doesn't allow pets in the apartment and anyway, Felix would be unhappy. But he's really been your cat since I left. He hardly looks at me when I come home now."

That was true, but Jackie wanted to make it official. She had Sharon's old room and now she had Sharon's old cat. She could erase the "part-time cat" in her diary, on the All About Me page.

"After you get out of school next year, are you going to Hollywood?" Jackie asked.

"That's my plan. If I have enough money. . . and the experience . . . and if I pass the test I took today!" Sharon said.

Her sister was going places, Jackie thought. Nothing could stop Sharon. College, beauty school, an apartment in Harrisonburg, a job as a hairdresser . . . the next year would go by quickly and then her sister would be off to California. In no time she would be Sharon of Hollywood, Hairstylist to the Stars.

And Jackie would still be home, going to high school.

"I wish I could go some place," she said wistfully. But what she meant was, she wished she could go to the same places her sister was going.

"You've just been to Richmond, what more do you want?" Sharon teased. "Listen, when I

165

get out to California, you can come visit me."

"Really?" A trip to Hollywood! That was even better than dinner in a French restaurant downtown.

Sharon forked Jackie's untouched fries onto her own plate. "It may be two or three years before I get out to California. Things don't always go the way you plan. But I *will* make it." Jackie never doubted her sister's ability or her willpower for a minute. "But I'll be coming home, too, as often as I can. You know, I miss you and the folks. I like being on my own, but I miss being at home, too. It's strange. Sometimes I feel like I'm caught between the two places and that I don't belong anywhere yet."

Surely her sister never had feelings of uncertainty, not Sharon who plowed through life full steam, impulsively, taking the corners too fast.

"It's true," Sharon said, reading Jackie's skepticism. "When I come home I stay in the guest room. The guest room! Can you imagine being a guest in your own house?"

"I suppose you'd like your old room back when you come home."

"No, it's *your* room now, the way you've fixed it up," Sharon said. "You belong there. Not me."

No wonder there had been so much friction between them whenever Sharon came home to visit. If Sharon moved into *her* room, Jackie would have felt strange, too, but Sharon was never home long enough to claim any territory of her own.

"That weird feeling will probably go away

166

when I get myself established," Sharon said.

"In your career, you mean."

"No, as my own person."

"I thought you did that when you left last summer," Jackie said.

Her sister smiled. "It's an on-going process, Jackie. It probably takes years. You're finding that out yourself, becoming your own person."

Jackie thought about the past year and decided that Sharon was right. Becoming her own person was not accomplished in a few months, even aided with a list. It couldn't be achieved by moving into another bedroom or assuming a different role. Or by taking a trip.

"I'm really sorry I cut your hair so short," Sharon said sincerely. "You know, I'd fail the exam if I could somehow put your hair back."

Only a true friend would make such an unselfish offer. A forever-friend, one who is there through thick and thin. Jackie had ripped up the Sister Pact in a fit of rage, but she merely destroyed a piece of paper. They were still bound by the Pact. And they always would be.

"Then you'd delay being Sharon Leigh of Hollywood, Hairdresser to the Stars," Jackie said. "And I want to come out to California and visit you. Besides," she added generously, "my hair will grow. At least it isn't orange."

"Oh, that poor woman. Reba absolutely butchered her," Sharon said, laughing. "I bet they fight all the way back to Lynchburg."

Jackie laughed with her. It had been quite a day, but at least they still could laugh. She gazed

167

out the window at the interstate. She had the odd sensation that they were back in their father's old car, driving up and down the driveway. The feeling of closeness was the same, only this time they had a real destination.

"Are you ready?" Sharon asked, picking up the check.

"Yes," Jackie said. "I'm ready." She laid a crisp new dollar on the table by her plate. The first tip she had ever given. The gesture made her feel like . . . her own person.

And she had thought of leaving the tip all by herself, without her sister coaching her. Maybe her life wasn't as out of balance as she thought. Sharon would always be her sister, her best friend, but she wouldn't remain at the core of Jackie's existence. Jackie had three good friends and a boy who liked her, sort of. She was in high school, where anything could happen. Though she still had a long way to go, Jackie felt she had come a long distance.

Sharon got up to pay the check. Jackie noticed that while her sister looked tired, she wore the glow of accomplishment. She felt a pang of sadness. Sharon would be going back to Harrisonburg to work this summer. And then she'd start another year at college. But her sister would come back and they would go places together. Around and around. Up and down.

Jackie took two free mint-flavored toothpicks from the dispenser by the cash register, one for each of them. Then they got in the car to drive the last miles home.

About the Author

CANDICE FARRIS RANSOM, born July 10, 1952, is a younger sister. Many of her stories, including the popular Kobie books, *Going on Twelve*, *Thirteen*, *Fourteen and Holding*, and *Fifteen at Last*, are based on her own experiences growing up. Ms. Ransom says, "My brain stops at about age fifteen. I'm a grown-up by default."

Raised in Centreville, Virginia, Ms. Ransom still makes her home there with her husband, Frank, and one cat.

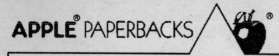

APPLE® PAPERBACKS

Pick an Apple and Polish Off Some Great Reading!

BEST-SELLING APPLE TITLES

❑ MT42975-2	**The Bullies and Me** Harriet Savitz	**$2.75**
❑ MT42709-1	**Christina's Ghost** Betty Ren Wright	**$2.75**
❑ MT41682-0	**Dear Dad, Love Laurie** Susan Beth Pfeffer	**$2.75**
❑ MT43461-6	**The Dollhouse Murders** Betty Ren Wright	**$2.75**
❑ MT42545-5	**Four Month Friend** Susan Clymer	**$2.75**
❑ MT43444-6	**Ghosts Beneath Our Feet** Betty Ren Wright	**$2.75**
❑ MT44351-8	**Help! I'm a Prisoner in the Library** Eth Clifford	**$2.75**
❑ MT43188-9	**The Latchkey Kids** Carol Anshaw	**$2.75**
❑ MT44567-7	**Leah's Song** Eth Clifford	**$2.75**
❑ MT43618-X	**Me and Katie (The Pest)** Ann M. Martin	**$2.75**
❑ MT41529-8	**My Sister, The Creep** Candice F. Ransom	**$2.75**
❑ MT42883-7	**Sixth Grade Can Really Kill You** Barthe DeClements	**$2.75**
❑ MT40409-1	**Sixth Grade Secrets** Louis Sachar	**$2.75**
❑ MT42882-9	**Sixth Grade Sleepover** Eve Bunting	**$2.75**
❑ MT41732-0	**Too Many Murphys** Colleen O'Shaughnessy McKenna	**$2.75**
❑ MT42326-6	**Veronica the Show-Off** Nancy K. Robinson	**$2.75**

Available wherever you buy books, or use this order form.

- -

Scholastic Inc., P.O. Box 7502, 2931 East McCarty Street, Jefferson City, MO 65102

Please send me the books I have checked above. I am enclosing $_____ (please add $2.00 to cover shipping and handling). Send check or money order — no cash or C.O.D.s please.

Name ——————————————————————————————

Address ——————————————————————————————

City————————————————— **State/Zip** ————————————

Please allow four to six weeks for delivery. Offer good in the U.S.A. only. Sorry, mail orders are not available to residents of Canada. Prices subject to change.

APP1090